traveling

light

a novelita

Candelora Versace

This is a work of fiction. Names, characters, businesses, places, events, locales, and incidents are either the products of the author's imagination or used in a fictitious manner. Any resemblance to actual persons, living or dead, or actual events is purely coincidental.

Different versions of some chapters have been previously published in *MEXICO: Sunlight & Shadows, Short Stories and Essays by Mexico Writers* ed. Michael Hogan, Linton Robinson, Mikel Miller; Egret Books, Guadalajara MX and *SOL: English Writing in Mexico* on-line literary journal from San Miguel de Allende, ed. Eva Hunter

Cover design: Sofia Howard
Cover art: Louise Roach
Author photo: Marc Howard

For my traveling companions, Marc and Sofia

CONTENTS

PROLOGUE

FEBRUARY 1994 SANTA FE, NEW MEXICO

Coyote points her nose in the chilly dawn, stands still for a moment, then trots slowly down Gypsy Alley. She passes the sleeping old casitas lining the narrow path, their painted mailboxes askew, and heads out onto Canyon Road. Santa Fe's legendary light is dim; cloud cover hangs heavy, and desolation colors the air.

Her nose once more uplifted, Coyote stops. She stands in the middle of the street and faces west, downtown. The tourist shops and galleries are closed; several have chains with large locks strung awkwardly through ancient front door handles. Sheets of plywood covering the windows are pasted over with hand-lettered fliers offering or seeking firewood, cheap rentals, and rides out of town. Faded and torn, they flutter in the winter wind. Several abandoned cars litter the narrow street, their windows broken, tires flat or missing, once-shiny paint faded and peeling.

Coyote smells piñon smoke—wood stoves and kiva fireplaces stoked against the snowless cold. And there is another scent in the air, the one she wants to follow. She trots down the road toward the Plaza, the old center of the small city. There is no movement on the street, no sound of traffic in the distance. She knows about cars and people, but there are none now, and she doesn't bother to stop when she comes to the Paseo.

Continuing across the empty thoroughfare, Coyote crosses the parking lot next to the long-abandoned old hospital, jumps the fence behind the cathedral, and cuts through its once lush tree-lined park. She follows a deserted Palace Avenue and finally stops on the Plaza. She is not the only one of God's dogs who has smelled death in the early morning winter air and followed its scent to the center of town.

PART I

1 Four Of Cups, Eight Of Swords

A shudder ran through Camelia, waking her from an uneasy sleep. She shifted in her cramped seat, sluggish mental synapses slow to catch up to her circumstances. She should be at work today, explaining why she hadn't returned after lunch yesterday; instead, she was spending an interminable day on various airplanes. With a hangover. Worse, she had been dreaming one of those unnerving parallel-reality dreams, so true in that vivid alternate-universe way that it filled her with unexpected regret.

A flight attendant made her way down the aisle, handing out warm cans of Coke. "Ice? Ice?" She bumped the ungainly cart into the aisle seats, hitting knees and ankles, the occasional elbow.

"¿Purificado, por favor? I mean, the ice?"

The young woman pursed her lips, handed her a Coke and a plastic ice-filled cup, and moved on. Camelia quickly drained her cup and refilled it. All that tequila yesterday, and did she and Melanie really eat nachos last night? By the time she had let Melanie talk her into dropping everything and going on what she knew even then was a fool's errand, they were both exhausted and edgy. How could she have let a quick lunch last well into the night? By then, she was only sober enough to know she should probably not have tried to drive home.

When her alarm went off this morning in the winter darkness, it had taken her several minutes to remember, still dressed in yesterday's clothes, that she wasn't going to her office but to the airport. Sunrise found her hastily filling a duffle bag with warm weather clothes, bottles and jars scooped up at random from the bathroom. She had no idea what she would find in there when she opened it up tonight. One thing she did know, however, was that as of dawn today, her husband had not yet returned.

The man in the next seat, uncomfortably close, was busy studying a Tarot card layout on his foldout tray. Taking in the colorful cards and his long hair, tie-dyed T-shirt, and fraying jean jacket, Camelia was also sure the leather cord around his neck held a small pouch under his shirt filled with tiny bones and feathers and little pieces of quartz. Oh, deliver me. She closed her eyes, shifting as far away from him as she could. All those planes—Albuquerque to Houston, Houston to Mexico City, Mexico City to Oaxaca—and she was stuck with another Santa Fe refugee as a seatmate.

She would have much rather been surprised to find she shared this flight with her neighbor, Claire, who frequently traveled to Oaxaca to visit her lover. Luis was an expert on the region's folk art; sometimes he gave lectures in Santa Fe and stayed with Claire for days or weeks at a time. Camelia couldn't keep track of their comings and goings, but oh how nice it would have been to sit with Claire today. Surely she would have had something wise to say to Camelia, although at this point, she wasn't sure if it mattered anymore.

"The Four of Cups is underneath the Lovers card, you see, and that gives you the support you need," her seatmate said suddenly, his eyes on his cards, his voice unmistakably directed at her. "The Eight of Swords is over the Lovers card, but the answer is simply to surrender to all you've created."

"Thanks; not interested," she said after a moment.

"You're going back to the source of your being, and it doesn't matter whether I tell you that or not."

"When I go back, I'll be going back to a fucking mess, that's what I'll be going back to." She rattled the ice cubes in her cup and turned to look out the window. She had left Santa Fe only this morning; she wasn't ready to think about what awaited her when she returned.

"I don't mean where you're going as in a *place*. I mean where you're going as in *your inner journey*." He held up his fingers and wiggled them, visual quote marks.

She remained silent and annoyed. He moved a card—a castle tower crumbling in flames—and tapped it a few times for emphasis.

"Change is internal. It doesn't matter if you change jobs or move or take a lover or run away. You'll just take your problems with you until you realize the burning tower is inside. You have to be completely empty in order to be fulfilled."

"Oh, spare me your New Age bullshit. Those cards are not going to tell me how to handle a damn thing."

"Look, I'm only the messenger." A whine crept into his voice. "I can't tell you how to handle it, I can just tell you what I see."

She slumped back in her seat. Too much flying, not enough to eat, and now this. Burning towers, inner journeys, empty vessels. She rummaged through her purse for some ibuprofen, trying to hide sudden tears.

Her seatmate moved a few more cards around and launched into an incomprehensible monologue on death and desire until a garbled voice over the loudspeaker interrupted him. The words were in Spanish, but Camelia knew what they meant and thanked God for it; she tightened her seat belt.

"There's one more thing you should know, and if you can't figure it out right now, don't worry." He gathered up his cards as the flight attendant rapped on his tray table. "The port you seek is within the emptiness. It's not out there, though; it's inside of you."

Emptiness. Oh, he had her there; it was the one thing she always ran away from, she knew, yet what did she find? Always more emptiness. Years ago, college had merely meant postponing inevitable decisions while partying, oversleeping, and scrambling for meaningless grades. She followed friends or lovers to different cities and fell into jobs that required little effort. And then suddenly she was past thirty and she wanted, fiercely, to be rooted. A man. A child. Yet the garden she planted just didn't take.

She rested her forehead on the window, watching the textures of Oaxaca rush upward to meet the plane as it touched the earth and came slowly to a halt. When she turned back, her seatmate had already left the plane.

The swirl of people around her hurried to waiting cars and taxis that filled the warm air with the smell of exhaust. Camelia found her duffle bag in a pile of luggage dumped on the sidewalk outside the airport and stood with it for a moment, unsure. Not particularly tall, still she towered over many of the older Mexicans, and it made her feel awkward and conspicuous. She thought again of Luis and Claire, making this trip regularly; they wouldn't look like tourists or feel so out of place. And then, she was almost a head taller than Luis as well; Claire, she had noticed, fit perfectly up against him, his arm always wrapped so protectively around her shoulders. Claire would of course feel right at home.

How lucky Claire was to be with Luis; good, steady Luis. Once upon a long time ago, before he even knew Claire and certainly long before Camelia found Michael, she had spent a particularly pleasant evening drinking at Casa Abuelita with him following one of his lectures. The next morning, she knew in her heart he would have loved her forever if she had let him, a fact that scared her to her bones. And so grateful was he to Camelia for subsequently introducing him to Claire, he had remained ever gentle with her.

Finally Camelia turned back inside with her duffle and slouched into a rickety plastic chair against the glass walls of the terminal. The throng of American tourists and Mexican businessmen ebbed and flowed around her. A surprising number of women wore traditional garb, all bright colors and intricate embroidery, which she had seen many times on both Claire and Melanie. Just as many, though, were decked out in suits and heels, looking like they had just come from Chicago. It was after three; any minute now, a daily afternoon puddle jumper would arrive to take her finally to Dos Palmas and the Hotel Paloma Blanca, the remote coastal escape belonging to Melanie and her husband Chris and apparently the source of endless strife between them.

Her singular assignment: find Chris Sullivan at the hotel and make sure Nico, their teenage son, was there with him. Melanie's frustration with the erratic phone service in southern Mexico had driven her to distraction. That she would send Camelia on a full day of travel just to accomplish what one five-minute phone call could have achieved seemed to Camelia a bizarre—and expensive— way to handle things. Was this how Melanie and Chris always operated?

Then again, how many margaritas had they had last night when they hatched this ridiculous plan? And now here she was, three flights done and one more to go, and she hoped against hope that Nico and Chris would be sitting at a table in the hotel's restaurant sharing some chicken mole when she got there. Then she would just spend a few days at the beach on her friend's dime, solve all her problems, and come home to a fresh start. Easy.

First, though, she had to avoid that asshole from the airplane, who now strode across the small terminal like he'd been there before. Four of Cups, Eight of Swords, empty ports; she was having none of it, thank you very much. She buried her head in her duffle bag for a minute, until she was sure he had left the building. Although the flower-laden airport was tiny—just a single glass-enclosed room looking out onto the parched runway—he either didn't see her or had wisely decided to leave her alone.

Camelia soaked up the warm February sun through the glass. If she thought she would use this time away from home to forget about having to face herself, she was out of luck. The Tarot guy was right about one thing. It didn't matter if she ran away for a few days or forever; her problems—and her own hand in creating them—came with her. Today was a little late to realize she had no clue why she was with Michael in the first place. Pushing him into marriage had been a ridiculous idea; their brief life together had barely begun before he started staying at his own apartment. What had she done? More importantly, she knew she had to ask herself why.

Thinking about the holiday season just past still stung. Everything she had tried to plan, based naively on tourism brochures from the hotel where Michael worked, fell apart at the last minute. He would call her at home from his own apartment, saying little besides, "Year-end report, you know that." Of course. His work deadlines always loomed; if he wasn't at his own apartment, he was at the hotel. Sometimes he even slept there, yet she refused to let simple facts sink in. Her holidays were a blur of bad television and lonely carryout.

And when Michael emerged from his deep winter hideaway and tried to make himself at home with her again, she'd ruined it with one simple sentence. She had no idea he'd respond that way. Her period had been late before; it was hardly a crisis, it would start in a day or so. And to be fair, he had made it perfectly clear during those awkward conversations she kept initiating last year that he had no interest in having kids. He was barely interested in being married. Perhaps he had only gone through with it in the first place because he was as terrified as she was not to.

Camelia stood and stretched; the little airport was quiet now. When her plane arrived, she'd join the other beach goers and fasten one more seatbelt, drink one more Coke. She sat back down, her duffle on her lap like a big pillow, and pressed her fingertips against her eyelids until tiny flashes of light sparkled in the darkness.

A fragment of the dream she had on the plane came back to her. In Santa Fe, they call Coyote the Trickster, but she was sure the dream meant death. Whenever she heard coyotes howling near her house, she knew their hunt had been successful.

Something had died, of that she had no doubt.

"Camelia?" Luis stood in front of her, a well-worn leather pack slung over his shoulder. "What are you doing here?"

She stared at him. It was as though he had materialized directly from the shimmer of heat waves bending the runway outside the glass.

"It's Nico," she blurted out finally. "He's gone; Melanie sent me to find him. I'm just waiting for the plane to go down there."

"Nico? What about Nico? I just saw him; he's with Chris at the hotel." Luis dropped his pack and sat next to her. "Why didn't Melanie just call?"

Camelia's throat tightened; her eyes filled.

"I'm so tired, Luis."

"Come," he said after a long moment. "I'm on my way home."

2 Women Disappear Here

Luis padded quietly into the kitchen. Camelia was already sitting at the table, her bare feet up on a chair, gazing out the window toward the village. The sound of young voices, fading in and out with the fragrant breeze, drifted up the mountain from Escuela para las Niñas, the girls' school down the road below his house. He could hear her humming along to a Spanish version of do-re-mi. She wore a wrinkled pink T-shirt left untucked over well-worn Levi's; he glimpsed orange polish on her toes. Several inches of silver bangles, some of them marked with turquoise, circled her wrists, crept up her forearms. Her hair was a riot of soft waves and tendrils. If it weren't for all her sharp angles—knees, shoulders, cheekbones—she'd look like a tropical flower. He held his breath for a moment, suddenly unprepared.

The dawn mist on the village below slowly disappeared, replaced now with the smoke from many outdoor kitchen fires. He could stay here all morning watching the familiar scene with her, pointing out various landmarks and sharing tales of life in the village, but her sadness permeated the room. He had no idea what was expected of him at this moment.

Perhaps he should just tell her that he'd already begun to worry about what to do with her. That her fragility frightened him. Oh, of course he wouldn't do that, any more than he would tell her that her lovely, painful presence was creating a disturbance in his carefully constructed private realm. That merely by sitting at his table in her pink T-shirt and her tears, she was lobbing bombs into his quiet refuge.

"You're not going to believe this," he said, his voice too hearty. "I actually fell out of my hammock last night. *Un oaxaqueño* who can't even stay still in a hammock. Disgraceful."

She smiled, and he pulled her without resistance through screenless doors out to the portal so he could demonstrate how last night he had attempted to arrange himself several times under a mosquito net in the hammock. He had given Camelia his room, which was equipped with its own mosquito net strung over the bed; she wouldn't even have noticed the midnight marauders.

"Big as horseflies," he said, climbing in the hammock and draping himself with netting. "Loud as chainsaws. They were incredible. Seriously, I have lived in a hammock all my life. That I would not be able to manage this simple task"—and at this moment he played the fool, swinging wildly, his limbs tangling in the net—"well, it doesn't speak very highly of my level of competency. I have spent too much time in *los Estados Unidos*. I suppose I will stay inside on the *banco* tonight." His grin faded. He could see how hard Camelia was trying, how badly she wanted to be cheered up.

"Oh, never mind." Abruptly he took her tinkling arm and steered her back into the big kitchen, releasing her to the sturdy table and its bird-eye view of village life. Yes, I am a foolish fool, *es verdad*.

"I'll make you some *chocolate con leche*." He lit the stove under a saucepan of milk mixed with pieces of the hard, spiced chocolate Oaxaca was known for. Of course he was not wrestling with the mosquito netting last night—he knew how to handle a few mosquitoes and a hammock, he knew who he was, Luis Sabio was no fool—no, he was fighting doggedly with himself over what to do, because he knew he had to do something.

He knew yesterday, as they drove up the rocky hillside to his house, singing loudly along with the radio so he would not hear the misery in her sighs, that she could not stay here with him, he could not stay here with her, he could not listen to another word about the ridiculous and completely pointless mess she had created in her life with all of her silly ideas about the way things ought to be and how carelessly she refused to see things as they were.

After finding sleep impossible last night, he had headed quietly back into the house and into his study. The light blinked on his answering machine: Claire, from early that morning, when he was still in Dos Palmas. She, in turn, had gotten a message from Camelia the night before, slurred and confused. "It sounds like she's coming to Mexico. Maybe you'll see her."

With a shaking hand, he had dialed Chris Sullivan at the Hotel Paloma Blanca, unmindful of the late hour. He knew Chris would be awake. Whether he would also be alone he could not say.

"What do you mean, she's looking for Nico?" Chris had answered the phone after only a couple of rings, his voice lively despite the time. "I called Melanie last night and told her Nico was here and that I'd get him on a plane back to Santa Fe as soon as I could. She was kind of tanked; she said she and Camelia had been drinking all afternoon at Casa Abuelita. *¡Que borrachitas!* But I told her I had the kid, I definitely told her. You were here this morning; you saw him, didn't you? I don't get what

Camelia was doing at the airport in Oaxaca today. That doesn't make any sense, *hermano*."

"I know, it's *loco*. What can I tell you? That's what she told me: Melanie bought her a ticket last night, told her to come find Nico. She put the fear of God in her, not to mention several margaritas. I don't know how the hell she got herself to Albuquerque so early this morning. Anyway, it sounds like she might also have lost her job and her . . . well, Michael, he split. A perfect storm, no? She's kind of a mess, but listen, she cannot stay here. Claire is coming in a few days. I can't . . . this won't work."

Luis had rubbed his eyes; he rarely stayed up so late. Deep quiet enveloped his house on the mountain, but it was not the same at the beach resort. Chris would be leaning across the bar, pouring mezcal for a college girl on break or maybe a newly divorced middle-aged woman, their arms brushing against each other, their eyes locking. *Ayii*, I know too much. His heart was heavy.

"By all means, put her on the plane and send her down here, that's what Melanie wanted," Chris said, a sudden edge to his voice. Luis could hear glassware clinking, women laughing. "I won't have to listen to all the messy details though, will I? Brokenhearted stories just depress me. I usually wind up drinking too much mezcal myself."

"Oh, *sí*, I know what you mean," Luis had said, gazing at a photograph on the desk of Claire, his Clara, Clarita. He ran his finger gently across the picture.

Just as he was ready to hang up, Chris spoke again. "Hey, didn't you and Camelia have a thing once?"

Oh, he should have lied, he should have sputtered and laughed at the absurdity of it. And how did Chris know anyway about that one night so long ago? Unless, of course, women, they tell each other everything. He was sure Melanie must know everything about everyone, and then of course so would Chris. And Melanie had not spared Claire—who of course then told Luis—the unpleasant details of what she put up with from Chris, Chris living at the hotel on the beach with an endless supply of young women on vacation and Melanie, stuck in Santa Fe raising their two kids on her own. Ah, me; bend or break, we do what we choose to do.

"Just once, a long time ago. But trust me, that's not what's happening here," he had quickly replied, a knot forming in his gut. "She's just . . . I don't know, she hit a wall; it has nothing to do with me. She'll get over it soon and head back home. She's not the type to fall apart for long. Melanie was probably right to send her down here. It's just, you know, I can't take care of her. She needs a break from it all."

"Ah, don't we all, *amigo*, don't we all," Chris said and hung up. Luís had spent the rest of the night sure he had just made the worst mistake possible on Camelia's behalf.

The chocolate began to bubble; its intoxicating aroma filled the room. Luis pulled out a chair from the table and sat next to Camelia. "You did a good thing coming here, trying to help your friend. I'm sure Melanie was very upset, not being able to find her son. But Nico is fine; he's safe with his father. You should go down to the beach anyway and see him with your own eyes if you don't believe me. Chris will take care of everything. You can relax, enjoy yourself." He handed her a cobalt-blue ceramic bowl of hot chocolate and dipped a sweet roll, *pan dulce*, into his own bowl before eating. A layer of light foam and crumbs remained on his mustache.

Camelia swirled her chocolate, inhaling its fragrance. "Michael doesn't know where I am," she said after a moment. "He might not even realize I'm gone. I know you think I was crazy for agreeing to let him keep his own apartment after we got married. Of course you were right. I don't know what I was thinking."

All this talk of people not being where other people need them to be tired Luis. He bit his tongue before he could begin a long-winded lecture about how wrong Michael had been for her from the beginning. If a man wants to keep his own apartment, he doesn't want to be married; that is that. He himself was just waiting for Clara to finish up her massage business in Santa Fe so she could move permanently to Oaxaca. He did not need to grow old rattling around in this empty house alone. They had a plan, not a fantasy. Look at Chris—why did he even bother to maintain the fiction that he was married? Marriage meant together; who didn't know that? Once you started bargaining with things like separate apartments, or living in separate countries, *Dios mío*, all bets were off. You either wanted to be with someone or you didn't. But he said none of it. She would have to figure it out her own way; everybody did. Eventually he took the empty bowls, put them in a plastic tub in the sink, and added a bit of liquid soap from an old bottle he kept on the counter.

"I will just be watering before Manuel and Ramón come; they are helping me with the trees." He took a battered straw hat from a hook on the wall, affixed it firmly on his head, and strode out, relieved at last to have something useful to do.

Camelia's eyes rested on the bottle of dish soap for a long moment after Luis left the room. Its milky whiteness against the stone wall behind it made it look like the subject of a still life. Cheery off-white tiles, each painted with a soaring blue bird, lined the countertop; a vast grouping of cast-iron cook pots and utensils, some of them long past the days of active use, hung from a row of iron hooks. Is it the devil one always finds in the details, or is it God?

She had been in no mood for the tour of his home Luis insisted on last night. Bone weary and sick at heart, all she could think of was the untethered darkness of sleep. Even so, she had followed along gamely while he pointed out the walls of local stone, the handmade furniture, the colorful woven rugs. Now she wandered again through the house, the quiet rooms dim away from the morning light. Folk-art masks were arranged neatly on a marigold wall; small sculptures and totems were scattered about, sharing space with stacks of books.

The house was much like Luis himself: spare and purposeful, elegant in its simplicity. A portable massage table folded against a wall in his study and women's sandals tucked neatly in the closet were the only signs that someone else also sometimes inhabited the space. Last night, Camelia had watched him dump the used dishwater in the garden. He told her he burned most of what little trash he couldn't recycle, and she could see by the stash of crumpled paper bags under the counter that he carried the same ones to the *mercado* every week.

All he wanted out of life, he said, was peace and quiet. His family, entrenched in noisy and sometimes violent Mexico City politics for a dozen generations, had scoffed at the impracticality of the remote site he had chosen to build his personal sanctuary. The land was barren and rocky but exceptionally private; he showed her where it butted up against government property on one side and an abandoned hacienda on the other.

Peace and quiet indeed. Camelia strolled onto the portal. Luis was out there somewhere, attending to the hundreds of trees he had planted with the results of a new well he had spent nearly six months drilling. Soon they would form a wall of greenery on the property line. Bougainvillea draped heavily from the curves of the arched portal; flowers of purple and red and pink ringed the house.

Camelia idly picked up some pink blossoms from the clay tile floor and took them back into the kitchen, dropping them in a blue bowl. With sudden inspiration, she dug around in her duffle bag until she found a tiny sewing kit, a giveaway from one of his company's resorts where she and Michael had once stayed. Her straw hat, somewhat crushed but not too damaged, was jammed in the bottom of the duffle. She sat in a time-softened *equipale* chair on the portal, watching Luis make his rounds through his mountaintop empire, and strung the bougainvillea blossoms with needle and thread. They came together easily, drying like tough pink paper. In no time, she had a chain long enough to wrap around the crown of the hat.

"I need to go to the *mercado* today. You can stay here and relax or come with me." Luis walked up to the portal from the yard, startling her; he took off his hat and wiped his brow. "I will get more tamales. When Clara's here, I do a lot more cooking, but when she goes back to Santa Fe, I tend to live on tamales."

"I love tamales, too." Last night's dinner had certainly been among the best she had ever tasted; she'd live on them, also, if she could find some that good at home. But the thought of leaving the cocoon of Luis's private retreat suddenly filled her with panic. "And I would love to go with you, any day but today. How about you fly, I'll buy?" She fished a wad of pesos from her pocket, hastily acquired yesterday in the Mexico City airport, and handed it to him.

He turned and left without a word, but she was sure he was relieved. She locked the front door behind him, even though she had already noticed no one could get within a mile of the house without being heard and seen from the back portal. Crime was not exactly a problem around here anyway, Luis had told her. No one was interested in his antique dance masks and ancient religious carvings. If they actually did come all the way up here and get in undetected, they'd probably take his toaster oven.

But Camelia had never been able to lose the habit of locking things up. She often found herself locking her car even when she was just jumping out for a moment—the gas station, the mailbox—and back in again. She did not think living in Santa Fe was supposed to be like that, but she knew better now.

When Camelia had first arrived in Santa Fe some years ago and settled into her rented casita, her new neighbor had given her a word of warning. "Women disappear here," Claire had said. "They find them in dumpsters or arroyos or in abandoned cars, or they don't find them at all." Although at first she thought Claire was just being overly paranoid, Camelia eventually realized her friend was right. Female bodies were found with alarming frequency, sometimes brutally unidentifiable.

"You used to hear it was a boyfriend or a husband who did it, like it couldn't just randomly happen to you," Claire had added as she packed her things for a trip to Oaxaca, a place she had been well acquainted with long before she met Luis. Claire's little house was as simple and serene as this one. Her massage table and oils, her herbs and remedies all were set up in a back room that gave the whole house an air of tranquility. Or perhaps it was just Claire herself who filled the space with peace.

"It seems like it's different now. It could be anyone, anytime. It's like a dark thing has moved in over the whole city. Sometimes when I make these trips to Mexico, I'm not sure I want to come back here anymore."

Now that she herself was here in Luis's world, Camelia understood exactly what Claire had meant. She felt herself breathe deeply in a way she hadn't for a very long time. Weariness settled in her. Letting the coolness of the empty house chase her outside, she stretched out lizard style on the hard ground, her face against the bone dry dirt. Tiny grains of sand and little stones were sharp against her rough winter skin. Prickly grasses tickled her wrists between her bracelets. She soaked up the heat from the land beneath her and likewise drew in the warmth from the sun on her back, feeling not unlike an ancient adobe brick.

She tried not to think of the two words—"I'm late"—that had sent Michael out of her house into the night and dropped her into Melanie's crazy scheme some two thousand miles away.

Maybe she would just stay here forever. She would lie here like a dozing iguana, occasionally opening one eye to keep watch on the road for Luis's car bringing its weekly load of tamales *con calabacitas* and mezcal and the tiny Mexican limes he called *limones* to drink it with. She could do the watering for him or be his caretaker when he went to Santa Fe. She would disappear into the city when Claire came or, even better, move into the crumbling hacienda next door.

She would get fit and strong walking up and down the mountain road and raise her child like one of the natives—gently, with lots of old women around. One day she would wake up and realize that she dreamed in Spanish and could speak it fluently. She would never see Michael or Santa Fe again. She would be happy.

Voices broke into the private house of her thoughts, and Camelia's heart stopped beating. So much for her theory of the early detection of intruders. She opened the one eye not hard against the earth to a pair of boots and jeans thickly caked with red dirt. Next to the boots stood another pair, similarly laden. Behind them, she spied the tines of a crude rake, a pickax with a rough wooden shaft, and the point of a well worn spade. Her heart, with a jump start, now beat so loudly in her ears she almost did not realize one of the men was speaking to her. His voice was a whisper.

"¿Señorita, señorita?"

Lizards don't smile; neither did Camelia, although she carefully turned her gaze upward. The man spoke again, his lips barely moving beneath a heavy brown mustache. Deciding finally that they did not intend to whack her with the garden tools but were here to work for Luis, she waved her sun-heavy hand at him and heard herself say, "*Soy amiga de Luis, señor. No hay problema. Muchas gracias. Estoy loca, es verdad.*"

For a moment it seemed all the birds of Mexico stopped their singing. And then the mustached man grinned uncertainly. The other, perhaps barely out of his teens, smiled, and they walked away to a corner of the property and started digging, the pickax and shovel hitting the earth in a rhythmic dance she felt vibrating beneath her. She heard them laugh and talk between themselves, and even though she once again closed her lizard eye, she knew they were looking at her. *Norteamericana loca. Es verdad.*

3 Luis Goes to el Mercado

Pan dulce. Tamales. Verduras. Cerveza. Limones. Frijoles. Luis went through his mental list several times, repeating it out loud as his old Bug wove its way down the mountain road. All that he knew—the sound of Camelia's bitter words of pain and regret, the way her fingers shook as she tried to cut a piece of fruit—conspired to distract him from his task at hand.

Pan dulce. Tamales. Cerveza. It's not right, thought Luis. It's not right to make a woman beg for love. How could that man, that Michael, her *husband*, not understand such a fundamental truth about the world? *Verduras. Agua. Limones.* He felt his concentration waver. The road down from his house to the first shacks of the villagers below had been carved out of the mountain with sweat and muscle and a few primitive hand tools. He had made the trip so many times he knew where every large rock, every deep rut, every fallen tree limb lay in wait for unsuspecting tires, yet he never got used to the continuous bouncing and jostling and swerving necessary to make it down safely. As always, when he reached the paved intersection, he was surprised to realize how good it felt to breathe again.

Heading onto the highway, he wiped the road dust from his eyes and listened to the passenger window, off its track, rattle and whistle in the wind. Traffic was heavy and not smooth. Every few minutes he, like everyone else, struggled with a gritty, jerking transmission to slow down at each of the *topes*. It was a challenge to stay alert, to keep his mind from wandering to his defeated houseguest. He was well aware that if he had any diversion of attention from driving, the impending speed bumps would lead not only to bone-grinding spinal shock but to the instant knowledge of possibly irreparable damage to the underbody of his car. He knew the location of each *tope* on the highway the way he knew the rocks and ruts of his mountain road. Nevertheless, mindful of his own distracted state this morning, he took special care to watch for them far in advance.

The sound of shrieking brakes and scraping metal as a bottled-water truck ripped its way over a *tope* ahead made Luis wince. He shifted, pressed the brake, and prepared for a long wait. The truck driver had decided to assess the damage to his truck while it was still in the middle of the highway. The process took several minutes and included the expert opinions of a number of now-stopped drivers from both sides of the highway. Luis sighed. Eventually, the truck driver began shaking hands all around, the other drivers returned to their vehicles, and traffic once again began to snake its way forward.

Cerveza. Agua. ¿Sandía? No, watermelon was not on his list today. He pulled onto a side street in Las Piedras for the *mercado del jueves*, affixed the heavy red security club onto the steering wheel, and locked the door. A skinny dog slept in the meager shade of the high curb, and three young boys lugging a metal tub filled with oranges struggled past him. He had a sack with him made of knotted string loaded with several wrinkled paper bags and a few colorful plastic ones. The broken sidewalk burned with the heat of day through his *huaraches*, and he wished he had remembered his hat.

Camelia. Oh, Camelia. What could he do for her except leave her alone? Luis jostled his way through the crowded market walkway, watching his step for small children and slippery smashed fruit underfoot. A young girl counted out a dozen fresh tortillas from her stack with the dexterity of a Las Vegas card dealer; into one of his crumpled bags they went.

Camelia's wedding had been a mistake; everyone in Santa Fe agreed. She's so smart about everything else, they all said; why is she so blind about him? And this whole business about wanting a baby. No, of course she didn't mention it last night when she arrived so unexpectedly, but he knew, he knew in the way she told him why Michael had suddenly left. She acted like it was no big deal, but he knew. She was already a few years into her thirties. *¡Dios mío!* Why hadn't she gotten that over with a long time ago? What a thing to have to push into a relationship at this time in her life, when instead she should just let herself enjoy falling in love.

He picked out a handful of *limones* and two sweet-smelling papayas, beginning his juggling game with the empty bags and the full ones, trying to get the food-filled bags into the string sack without pushing the empty bags further out of reach. He stood in the crowded aisle calmly transferring bags and repacking them, all the while impervious to the steady stream of people passing on either side of him, bumping him with their full shopping bags.

He was already sure that night long ago, even with all that tequila and Camelia's playful advances, that she would start getting crazy about having a baby soon enough if he stayed with her. She wouldn't even notice the difference in their ages, would have taken it for granted that the, what, almost twenty years between them meant nothing, when to him it meant everything about who he was in his life now. "*Muchas gracias*, but the family thing was over for me a long time ago," Luis had said to her at what he hoped was an opportune moment, perhaps when they were leaving Casa Abuelita? Or on arriving at her casita?

Somewhere along the line, he was sure of it, he'd told her. "Yes, I have a son, one son, he's a man now," he had said. "He works in Mexico City with his *abuelo*, my father; he holds some important government position. What is it they say sometimes in Santa Fe—round parents, square children? Perhaps *my* grandson will come and live with me on the mountain in Oaxaca." She had laughed, he remembered now. She had laughed—but he could see in the flicker of an eyelash, a tapping of a fingernail, that she was shifting her mental strategies and calculations. By dawn, she had brushed off their lovemaking as a tequila-induced adventure never to be repeated.

He stood still in the aisle for a moment to assess his shopping progress. Every Thursday he came to this market; if he needed something else at another time, he had to go to a different village. The Monday market was another twenty miles from his house but he wound up there almost every week because yes, there was always something else he had wanted on Thursday but couldn't carry, his arms already filled with bags of greens, boxes of milk, the precious sack of fresh tamales.

What is the nature of the healing process for the broken heart, he mused, as he directed one of the merchants to weigh out the black turtle beans Claire loved. Claire, his Clara coming back to him and their quiet aerie soon; Clara, with her soft doe's eyes and crystal laugh. *She* would know what to do for Camelia. She was a healer, after all; her hands had that touch that went beyond the mere massage. Sometimes heat came from her palms the way it had from his own *abuela*'s hands when he was a boy and feeling sick. But heartbreak? Then again, that he did not know if Claire could help at all.

Do you treat the victim like one who is sick, with warm soups and soft words and many hours of sleep? Perhaps instead you educate, look for reasons, talk of lessons, hope to stave off the almost inevitable repetition down the road. Maybe Camelia will just drink herself into a stupor and doze in the hammock before going down to the coast. Not a bad prescription, he reflected, although it never worked well for him. With no small thanks to Camelia herself that night long ago, he had finally figured out that drinking to excess was bad for his personality. It made him susceptible and hopeful. He had acted foolishly and without caution before under the spell of the locally made spirits. Tequila in Santa Fe was just as dangerous, if not more so; about that Luis had no illusions.

He asked for tamales with *calabacitas*, *mole rojo*, and the sweet ones with *canela*, cinnamon. *Pan dulce* from the *panadería* across the street and then back to the car, with a stop at the bodega on the highway for beer and water, and his errand would be complete.

I will cast my net wide, he decided. If she wants to talk, I will talk. If she wants to sleep, I will tell Ramón and Manuel to work on the other side of the house so it's quiet. If she wants to drink, I will leave the mezcal where she can find it. If she wants to kill herself, I will stop her, hold my arms around her, and say the rosary until the sweat pours off my brow and my fingers leave blue marks on her arms. It will have to be enough.

4 *Traveling Light*

Camelia woke in her cave of netting with the sensation of having fallen into the bed from a very great height. It seemed for a moment as though a loud noise had startled her awake, and she paused without breathing until she determined that no, there had been no gunshot, no thunderclap, no explosion in the distance. She was merely awake, whereas before she had been asleep. She pulled on a tank top and a pair of khaki shorts, unworn since last summer and not as comfortable as she'd hoped, and made her way barefoot to the kitchen. A note from Luis on the kitchen table, held down with a small rock, fluttered in the light morning breeze.

Luis told her the table had once, a hundred years ago, belonged to the village butcher, and its surface was pitted and scarred from a thousand daily strokes of the cleaver. Ants made their way carefully across the treacherous terrain; she brushed several off the note to read it. "Have gone to town to pick up mail, etc. I can drive you to the airport tomorrow when I go to pick up Claire. *Lo siento.* Stay as long as you wish." I'm sorry too, Camelia thought. She had no desire to darken their perfect love nest.

Lurking about in Luis's orderly house, Camelia felt excessive and obtrusive, even though for perhaps the first time in her life she was traveling light. Luis, with his single bar of natural olive oil soap resting on a small block of stone on the bathroom sink and his two pairs of worn *huaraches* neatly standing at attention inside the front door, had mastered the art of living simply. His house was rich—luxurious even—in its sense of space, its lack of clutter, its feeling of openness. And yet, some of his furniture was more than rustic; it was decrepit. *Trastero* doors were held together with string, table legs were crooked, chairs threatened to give way if you leaned back too far. If he were to move the furnishings to a folk art gallery in Santa Fe, he could live in Mexico for years on the prices they'd fetch. She knew he knew that, too.

She looked out the window facing the village below and felt a sudden urge to divest herself of all her belongings. Having already left behind a job, a home, and a husband, perhaps she should complete the process by discarding the rest of the baggage she'd brought with her. She'd distribute her clothes to the older girls down the mountain and her makeup to the whores on the backstreets of the city, give her money to the gardeners for their families, feed her Spanish phrase book to the fireplace. Or she could do nothing, because nothing matters anyway, she thought grimly, staring at the trails the ants had worn in the table. She would still feel useless and unnecessary.

The house retained the cool of the last hours of night; chilled, she stepped out to the portal and then onto the already baking earth. The steady *chink-chink-chink* of iron against stone let her know without seeing them that Ramón and Manuel had started early at their daily Herculean task of converting the barren property into an oasis. The young girls' singing practice at the *escuela* down the mountain had already begun; her throat tightened at the sweetness of their song and she went back inside.

Last night, she'd told Luis she had yet to cry over Michael, but once she did, she probably wouldn't stop.

"Maybe you should stand out in the garden so my flowers and trees can benefit from the ensuing flood," he had said, a tentative smile curling under his mustache. His warm brown eyes, so wary earlier in the day, were soft in the dim evening light, and his teeth, small and uneven, were bright between his mustache and beard. He had started to put the lid on the jug of warm, woody mezcal, looked at her for a long moment, and then very deliberately placed the lid back on the counter next to the bottle.

"*Medicina.*" His tone was stern. "Sip." He had headed off to sleep, this time on the banco in the living room. Heeding his words, she had left the jug untouched when she went to bed.

This morning, her eyes still dry, she knew she had already grieved enough. She had cried so many times over so many different little heartbreaks with Michael, why should she have any tears left? She didn't miss him, not even his body at night, tucked in behind her spoonwise so she could sleep with the comforting knowledge that her back was covered. It had been too long since they had slept that way.

At this moment, she didn't miss Santa Fe, either. It had become nothing but congested streets and rude tourists. No one seemed to know how to drive properly. Empty beer bottles lined the washboard dirt road to her house. She certainly didn't miss sitting in her dark little office tucked behind the crumbling old museum of the Palace of the Governors, a dank room that was stifling in the summer and cold in the winter. She spent her days poring over countless applications from desperate artists hoping for nonexistent government funds; she stuffed the pages into drawers, piled them under her chair, brought them home and forgot about them. If she left Santa Fe for good, she wondered, was there anything she *would* miss?

She decided to make a list, inaugurating it with a short drink of mezcal from the jug still on the kitchen counter and offering a toast to *las niñas* down the mountain. It tasted of charred desert flowers, of smoke and sand; the lime was tangy on her tongue. She found a crumpled paper bag in a hanging basket to write on and a stub of pencil hiding in a drawer of cutlery. Settling into a comfortable *equipale* chair at the ancient slab of a table, after many moments of silence, she began to write.

"The flowers in front of the El Rey Inn in the summer," she said aloud, her voice tentative in the empty room. "The boot repair place behind Big O Tires. The chocolate cake at the Zia, the green chile cheese fries at Baja Tacos, the sweet iced coffee at the San Marcos Café." As the list grew, she was surprised at how the smallest details of her life in Santa Fe captivated her. The full moon rising quickly from behind the Sangre de Cristos, the coyotes calling and laughing among themselves deep in the night. And the scents: Russian olive trees blooming in June, chiles roasting in the fall. There was piñon smoke downtown during the winter and the intoxication of lilacs and wisteria in the spring.

Another part of Santa Fe, however, was nowhere to be found on her paper-bag list: art gallery openings, so turgid and superficial; the prices on restaurant menus and the high cost of rent; the "Santa Fe Style" costumes in the windows lining the Plaza and worn by clueless tourists. Also missing from the list was Michael's dimpled smile, how good he looked in red, and his capable ways around her kitchen. She dropped the pencil on the table and prowled around in the tiny refrigerator for more of the fresh tamales they had eaten last night.

After carefully rinsing her dish and returning it to the cupboard, she made one more pass at the jug, poured a couple fingers' worth and drank it quickly, ignoring the sipping rule and forgoing even the *limón* to cut its sharp edge. Camelia would let the earthy warmth of the mezcal seduce her. It could unlock the secrets inside of you, so legend went, or make you blind—you never knew which it would do. The risk seemed worthwhile at the moment. She retreated to the hammock and closed her eyes.

As she hoped it would, the crudely made liquor did its job, taking her down to that place far beyond where lizards doze, where instead dreams lie broken like so many sun-dried bones and hearts are fragile, scarred by the rusted barbed wire they're wrapped with. Camelia journeyed in a deep mezcal dream in which she was counting months, counting years, until she went back ten years—ten years ago this month, to be precise. She was calling all her girlfriends on the phone, one after another, her fingers absently toying with the nubby orange fabric of her thrift-store sofa cushions as she unsuccessfully tried to find someone who would give up a Saturday to accompany her to the women's clinic and shield her from the demonstrators whom she knew would line the entryway. Someone who would hug her and maybe make her some soup after and stay with her while she cried all night, knowing it would not be a night to be alone. Which, anyway, she was.

Camelia had rarely given thought to the child she would otherwise have today, beyond counting every spring how many years it had been since she had made that unhappy but necessary choice. Now, as she swayed suspended in the colorful hammock, she hazily saw a little boy standing off to one side, throwing pebbles at the flies. He was just far enough outside her field of vision to make her second-guess his presence. But she did see him. He wore a striped T-shirt and jeans; he was neither tall nor short for his ten years. His hair was dark, his cheeks, freckled, and he was gone in an instant as her vision blurred.

He was not the one she expected to see. Not a grown child. There had been instead an infant hovering around the edges of her dreams at night and in daylight, the want of a baby in her arms gnawing at her heart until her very skin burned with the knowing that no matter what was happening in her life, there was a child who was supposed to be in it. Tears were hot on her cheeks.

Don't come now. You know I want you, but if you come, you have to bring a father too, one who wants you, one who will stay. You find that one and keep him here with us, and then I will welcome you with blue flowers and hummingbirds and soft, wet kisses on your perfect little ears.

Finally, dreamless, she slept. And then her legs were burning in the sun, and she heard Luis moving about in the kitchen. He came up behind her and put a steaming cup of strong coffee in her hands, loaded with milk and sugar the way she liked it, though she couldn't recall telling him so. He pulled a wooden chair from the kitchen table out to the portal and sat beside her. Ramón and Manuel had gone home for their midafternoon meal and siesta; they would return before sunset and work until dark, and then come back again in the morning before the dew was dry on the stubbly grass.

"When I was growing up, I had an uncle who was considered the family's disgrace," Luis said after a few moments, his eyes on his garden and the dry desert sky beyond it. "He had renounced the family's money and connections and went to live in the mountains among *los indios*. I spent a year with him when I was fourteen. My family sent me to him because I had run away from home so many times. They thought if I saw how he lived, with almost nothing, I would learn my lesson, return to school, and prepare myself for some arranged government appointment in Mexico City and the straight life of a productive citizen."

He sipped his coffee. She swayed gently in the hammock.

"Tío Esteban taught me many things, especially about how to live with very little. More importantly, he taught me why. 'Do not do anything you do not want to do,' he told me. 'Life is long, too long to spend it doing what you hate. Do what is right and clean and just. It doesn't really matter what you do, just as long as you do it well and you treat other people right.'"

On the far edge of the property, a *campesino* with a burro trudged steadily down the mountain road, a load of firewood perfectly balanced on the animal's back. The heat hung heavy in the air, rich with the scent of *mole*, its seductive blend of bitter chocolate and chile rising subtly up from the valley. Camelia's limbs felt like stone, while another part of her, wispy and cloud-like, seemed to drift somewhere above the hammock. She watched as it floated toward the ceiling of the portal above her and then vanished. Luis swatted at a mosquito on his arm.

5 When Luis Sleeps

Luis snored, his mosquito netting draped over him like a wedding veil. Though he had been nervous when Camelia first arrived, knowing now that she would be leaving in the morning brought him some peace. He was comfortable enough on his banco in the living room to sleep deeply. And when he sleeps deeply, Luís always said, he dreams.

In the milky predawn light, she moves naked through the house like a disembodied spirit and makes her way across the back portal, leaving the door open behind her. The cold scrubby grasses and sharp stones stab her tender feet, but she steps heavily, as though she crushes glass with every step. As she walks down the sloping yard to the line of young trees, she feels deep within her what she has been waiting for: the warm path of rich red blood gently making its way down her leg.

She finds a level patch of earth and brushes it clear. She sits cross-legged, her hands on her knees, and watches the sky slowly lighten. The red line on her leg dries to brown, marks her, points toward the sun. She feels the sticky droplets collecting beneath her, soaking into the hard ground, drenching it, blessing it.

She touches the blood with her fingertips, lets her heart fill with grief, drags jagged red lines across her emptied womb. She lies back on the ground and sobs, her body shaking so violently the earth trembles around her, her tears forming a river running down the mountain, her cries of rage and heartbreak waking the coyotes sleeping among the rocks above her. They join her, keening and wailing, until the sound reaches the heavens and the clouds come forth and crash together and unleash such a rain as has never been seen before during the dry season in Oaxaca.

"¡Señor, señor!"

Luis struggled to pull himself off the banco, head heavy, eyes gritty. His dream still held him for a moment, then slipped away like fog. Manuel, the young gardener, was calling to him from the open back door. He held his dripping straw hat in his hands; his boots were muddy.

"¡Señor, es su amiga, la norteamericana loca!"

Wide awake now, Luis slipped into his jeans and *huaraches* and ran out the door behind Manuel, profoundly amazed to see rain. Ramón walked slowly up the hill, carrying Camelia in his arms. Her pale, naked body was streaked with mud and, he could tell clearly even from this distance, blood. Rainwater trickled from Ramon's mustache.

"¡Ayii, Madre de Dios!" Luis said under his breath and led Ramón into the bedroom. He knew how the man must have struggled to make the decision even to touch Camelia, let alone bring her back to the house. He could imagine the two of them arguing about who would carry her, knowing that one of them would have to do it and neither would want to. As Ramón unfolded her from his arms, Camelia curled into a fetal position on the bed.

"Muchas gracias, mis amigos. Yo la cuidare. No es loca. Esta enferma, enferma del corazón," he told them. Not crazy, just heartsick—as if that somehow were an easier burden. Could he take care of her now, as he so solidly assured them? He put an arm around Ramón for a moment before

sending them both home for the day. "*Que Dios los bendiga,*" he told them both as they hurried out the door. They did not look back. And oh, dear God, how we need your blessings this day, Luis thought, as a streak of lightning lit up the dark room.

Camelia sobbed quietly. Luis waited for his heart to return to its normal pace before he made a move. After a few minutes, he brought a towel and began to dab at the blood, the dirt, Camelia's rain-soaked skin. Thunder shook the windows, and again he marveled at the unusual weather. He stroked her sodden hair, her long, dark curls catching in his fingers. He watched as her breathing slowed; he dried her tears.

"I will make us some coffee," he said when he saw her wiry body relax muscle by muscle, limb by slender limb. The crisis is past, he thought. Please, God, let it be done.

"I must have been walking in my sleep," Camelia said when he put the hot mug in her hands. Her eyes did not seem quite right to him; he wasn't sure if she was not still asleep. But he was not so surprised. This was, after all, Oaxaca, land of the Cloud People. His *tío* had always told him that what was dream—and what was not—often confused the uninitiated.

And oh what a scare she must have given Ramón and Manuel. He shook his head and sighed. He had heard the word "*¡Bruja!*" muttered under their breath as they left, and he dreaded what would come next. They were heading for the village church, he knew. The story of the crazy witch at Luis Sabio's house would be all over the village before noon. He was already misunderstood; a lone, educated man choosing to live separated from his family and from village life, with a *norteamericana* who visited him often and sometimes mingled during village celebrations but would not marry him and had no children. And now this—how could he even begin to explain this?

Camelia had wrapped herself, shivering, in the sheets. "Claire comes today!" she said suddenly, looking at him, snapping into focus. "Oh, I've made such a mess of your bed. I need to go find Chris anyway. And Nico. I should get out of your way." She didn't move.

Ayii, maybe she is *loca*, Luis thought. He watched the rain out the window. He couldn't speak. Yes, go down to the beach, take your tears and your pain and your enormous love away from here, where all I want is a simple life, uncomplicated, without worry for how my brothers treat my sisters. Go, free me of this devastating sense of uselessness. He turned to face her.

"You have been so good to me, Luis," she said, her eyes on the steam rising from her coffee. "Somehow you always seem to know exactly what I need. You can't ever know how much it has helped me to be here these few days."

Mea culpa, mea culpa, stay as long as you like. "I can't do anything else for you, *chica*. I have to pick Clara up at the airport this afternoon; she left Santa Fe last night and stayed in Mexico City. You can take the next plane out to Dos Palmas if you want or, you know, maybe just go home. Maybe go back to Santa Fe and sort it out with Michael sooner instead of later." There was still the shadow of a streak of blood along her cheek like a red tear, stigmata. He reached over to wipe it off. "You know, you can do whatever you want."

"Home. That's a good one," she said, tugging the sheets more tightly around her. "It's just a short flight to Dos Palmas, isn't it? I think I need to be on the beach. What do you think?"

"What do I think? I think it'll take me a week to convince Ramón and Manuel to come back. I think you've cried more tears than any man deserves. I think a few days on the beach will give you a nice tan to go home with." His fingers absently played with the edge of the sheet, faded lavender, a favorite of Claire's. I think I will miss you.

"God, what a mess. I'm so sorry, Luis, I am so, so sorry. Oh, poor Ramón!" She started to laugh, and he gamely laughed with her until he saw another tear escape. He took the coffee mug from her hand and put his arms around her while she cried, her damp head buried in his shoulder, her tears warm as blood on his neck.

6 *Claire: Enough*

Usually when Claire arrived for one of her frequent visits, their steadfast ritual was to hurry downtown before everything closed up for the afternoon so she could fill the house with flowers. It was always a joyous excursion, rushing through the *mercado* as the merchants and farmers were closing up their stalls, waving and trailing *"¡Buenas tardes!"* behind them. They would navigate their way through the serpentine aisles, stalls bulging with *huipils* and *huaraches*, colorful tables laden with baskets of spices and dried chiles of every size. Once in the flower area, they'd search for her favorite gladiolus and tuberoses, hoping there would be some left and taking whatever colors remained, as many fragrant bunches as the two of them could carry.

But today, she and Luis drove from the Oaxaca airport with little spoken between them. There had been just that brief intersection with Camelia, who hurried on to the little plane with barely a glance back at them. Claire heard herself begin to chatter about the cold weather in Santa Fe; her words quickly died on her tongue. She sat against the passenger door and looked at Luis in silence for many minutes. Like an abandoned house, he was closed to her, vacant.

"I went to Las Piedras on Thursday," Luis said, his eyes on the road. "I have food at the house; we don't really need to go to the zocalo."

Her throat closed, and as the long minutes passed she could feel something unmistakably die.

"Oh, if you don't mind, I'd really like to get some flowers, Luis."

He managed the afternoon traffic without comment, pulling up to a parking space just outside the entry of the *mercado*. Claire ran inside without waiting for him to follow.

She buried herself among the basketry and leatherwork in the first stall she came to. As if she had fallen flat on her back and the wind knocked out of her, it took several minutes of careful, practiced steadying to will her constricted muscles to release, to cajole her lungs into breathing, her heart into beating. Luis came up behind her and wrapped his arms around her shoulders and held her tight. They stood there without speaking as the *mercado*'s bustling rhythms slowed to its midafternoon quiet.

They collected their flowers in silence and drove up Luis's road as though in a trance. The sun seared the dusty landscape; Claire saw everything in stark relief. As in Santa Fe, the high, clear air played tricks with sunlight and shadow, but today in the mountains outside Ciudad Oaxaca, she saw only a hard edge of pain etched into her dry surroundings. And then she saw the smoke.

"Luis?"

They rounded the last curve of the long driveway up to the house. Ramón and Manuel were stoking a fire in the old oil barrel Luis often used to burn trash; she was sure she saw the edge of her lavender bedsheets hanging outside the rim. He stared out the windshield at the two men, their faces grim in the heat and smoke. Claire opened the car door and threw up on the hard dirt.

He said he didn't sleep with her. He insisted he did not touch her. He said nothing happened, nothing at all between them, except that Camelia had cried a lot. He told Claire about meeting Camelia at the airport on Wednesday, just as she, Claire, had predicted; about every meal they ate and every glass of mezcal he drank. He told her of going by himself to the village *mercado* on Thursday and going into town on Friday morning. He was calm as he explained that of course he had given her their bed and slept on the banco himself—"Right there, my Clara, there is my mosquito net on the floor, that is where I slept. I have nothing to hide from you."—and that apparently Camelia's moon blood had started while she slept last night.

"We had a freak thunderstorm this morning, look around, the ground is still wet." He ran a hand over his mustache several times; she saw a light film of perspiration on his forehead. "I put the soiled sheets out on the portal with plans to take them to town later in the week to wash. After I left to go to the airport, Ramón and Manuel apparently took it upon themselves to clean up what they must have thought was merely trash."

Claire listened without comment. He kissed her, tentatively and tenderly. "Come, *querida*. Let's rest; it's been a long day."

They put fresh sheets on their bed together and held each other through the hot afternoon. When the sun went down, she awakened, groggy, and went into the kitchen. The huge bundle of gladiolus and tuberoses they had collected at the Mercado de Flores still sat in the sink. Their musky scent had permeated the room all afternoon, but it had not been enough to clear the air. She stood in the center of the room and knew. Something was not right.

Claire was not a jealous woman; she was not a suspicious or untrusting woman. She and Luis were as one in the best ways: they were independent of each other yet so deeply connected that neither of them considered even the possibility of someone or something upsetting their harmonious balance. And yet. The very air in the house vibrated with . . . something. It was as though even the molecules had somehow been disturbed.

Luis came in to the kitchen; he pulled a plate of sweet *canela* tamales from the refrigerator and set it on the table along with a couple of heavy glass tumblers and the bowl of *limones*. The jug of mezcal was on the counter; he poured an inch in each glass and gave her one.

Again, she had to ask him again.

He sat across from her at the table, his head in his hands.

"What I don't understand is why you can't just tell me, why can't you give me a straight answer, Luis?"

"I cannot tell you because I do not know."

"You don't know? You don't know what happened? Or you don't know why you can't tell me what happened?"

"I told you what happened. Nothing happened, everything happened, I don't know what happened. It doesn't matter, Clara. I. Don't. Know. I don't know how to stand things back up right, I don't know why everything is upside-down." His voice was unsteady. "I see Camelia in the Oaxaca airport, and three days later it is as though my skin has been turned inside out."

She tried to be calm. She breathed fully, grounding herself, connecting to a thread deep in the core of the earth and drawing it up into the bottoms of her feet; she felt the thread travel through her legs, up along her spine, and out the top of her head. She closed her eyes in a conscious effort to hold herself in one piece. Of course nothing had happened between Luis and Camelia; she knew that to be true.

But much as Claire liked Camelia, she was also wary of her. Camelia shared personal information rather freely, but she had that particular kind of callousness that came with being young and, until fairly recently, single. Other people's hearts didn't seem to matter so much to her.

And Claire was no fool. One morning a few years ago, she had stopped by Camelia's house to drop off a misdelivered letter and there she met Luis. In the span of time it took to have one cup of coffee with them, she understood more than either Camelia or Luis could have explained. Claire took Luis back to her house to show him the baskets she had been collecting on her trips to Oaxaca; within days they were inseparable.

He put the tamales back in the refrigerator and left her alone, but the longer she stayed in the kitchen, the more restless he became. She swirled the mezcal in her glass. If only she could unravel the tangles of the day, she could create order within her heart. She could hear Luis shuffling around the house, walking back and forth to his study, pretending to be working at one project or another while he waited for her to come back to bed.

He had said, "I don't know." He had said, "It doesn't matter." She dragged a fingernail along the fissures in the tabletop. The windows behind her were black, but the kitchen was brightly lit, unusually so. Mosquitoes lazily buzzed nearby; her ankles were already on fire, and the fat bastards were so drunk they could barely fly anymore. Her bag sat on the floor where Luis had hastily dropped it when they arrived that afternoon. It looked almost as though it might pick itself up and head back out the door on its own.

She gazed at the kitchen she had spent so much time in over the last few years. Everything was in exactly the same place it always was. Nothing was missing, nothing had changed.

Except, of course, everything.

Luis came back in to the kitchen, turned off all the lights save the one over the kitchen table where Claire sat, and ran water in the sink for the flowers they had all but forgotten earlier. He stood there in the dark with his hands in the cold water, moving the stems around a bit. Finally he spoke.

"Clara. Do not be angry with me. I have done nothing to hurt you." She felt her eyes fill. "You know I did not touch her. And you know that I love you. But I cannot say that I did not feel anything for her while she was here. Perhaps it was just the feeling I would have for a wounded bird on the portal, I don't know. But now she is gone, and you are back, and I want to believe the world will shift back into its normal orbit again. I hope you will forgive me for being a man with a soft heart."

He went to the table and stood in front of her, his arms at his sides, dripping water onto the floor.

It was enough, she knew. It had to be.

PART II

7 *It's Not Complicated*

Determined to pull herself together and stumbling only once on her way up the metal steps, Camelia boarded the puddle jumper that would take her finally to Dos Palmas and Chris and Nico. The drama of the early morning had exhausted her, but at least one complication had resolved itself under Luis's gentle care. Maybe by the time she got home the rest of her problems would have magically dispersed themselves as well.

The flight attendant, in stiletto heels and tangerine miniskirt, busied herself during the takeoff lighting a cigarette and chatting with the pilot. Camelia watched them through the cockpit's open door. She wondered if shattering into pieces across the mountains of Oaxaca was an option for resolution. There were three other people in the tiny cabin, but none of them appeared to be armed with Tarot cards or other nonsense, and she had the row of seats to herself. She arranged her sandaled feet on top of her duffle; obviously, no one was going to tell her to stow her bag.

The plane rattled and throbbed as it cruised low over dense greenery. Melanie and her family's problems had receded into the background while Camelia was in Oaxaca with Luis, yet soon enough she'd be at the Hotel Paloma Blanca as their guest. No longer was she sure about anything she had previously believed when it came to the Sullivans. In all of Melanie's drama she hadn't mentioned Rayne, Nico's sister, at all. What else was going on that Melanie hadn't told her?

A half hour later, the noisy plane began its sharp descent over the coastline. She tightened her grip on the hard plastic armrests and gritted her teeth. From her perch at the window, it looked for all the world like they were going to land on a streak of azure water she spotted between the greenery, or perhaps crash into a dense jungle of palm trees. Moments later, her body still vibrating from the engine's hum, she stepped off the plane to find the flowers of an eternal summer surrounding the diminutive Aeropuerto de la Costa, numero 4. She stood in silence; she had no idea what she was doing here.

The other passengers piled their luggage into the back of an old green station wagon parked close to the plane, an obviously hand-painted "Dos Palmas Servicio de Taxi" barely visible on the door. The driver, clad entirely in wrinkled khaki, beckoned to her to put her bag in with the others. He stood in the sunlight with his back to the little group, an old Raiders cap pushed back on his forehead and a toothpick clenched in his silver teeth, waiting with infinite patience as they arranged themselves in the car. Camelia pushed a dusty pile of mangled road maps and curled magazines off the front seat and settled herself in, shuffling her feet around an empty beer bottle.

"Oh my heavens, isn't this cozy," the older woman in the back seat said as she struggled to find a seat belt in the crowded car. The driver finally got in and gunned the car around the tarmac without warning. "Whoo-hoo! Isn't this grand?" she continued. "Eddie, doesn't this just remind you of that time in Baja when we hadn't even gotten the doors closed and we went round and round?"

The driver glanced in his rearview mirror at the passengers. Though his face remained impassive, Camelia sensed a shadow in his eye, a twitch in his jaw muscle. Suddenly he turned to her and said quietly, "Señor Chris, he is anxiously awaiting your arrival. However, he has another engagement this evening and probably will not see you until tomorrow morning. Until then, he hopes you to enjoy your stay and to feel free to have a lovely dinner in the hotel restaurant." An obvious leer curled around his teeth.

"I'm a friend of Señora Melanie." She turned away from his unpleasant chuckle, wondering how long *had* it been since Melanie had been back to Dos Palmas. The taxi veered off the highway without warning and rattled down an unpaved roadway, cut as though with a single machete through opulent jungle growth. Finally, she spied a mere sliver of sandy beach up ahead. Melanie had often said it was Mexico's last few miles of undeveloped coastline and she hoped to keep it that way.

The taxi jerked to a stop, although it appeared to Camelia they were nowhere near anything that might be a hotel. But when the others began gathering their things, she too hopped out quickly and grabbed her duffle bag from the back. Her protestations of "No, *gracias*" were unnecessary; the driver made no move to assist her or the other passengers with their bags. Suddenly he shooed them along with a stern "*Aquí, aquí,* this way, this way" and led his charges into a barely visible break in the greenery. Just as Camelia shouldered her duffle and prepared to follow, Nico appeared in the crude path in front of her. Part boy, part man, he was almost six feet tall, clad in loose black jeans, an REM T-shirt, and beat-up flip flops.

"Nico, I'm so glad to see you!" She dropped her duffle and threw her arms around him; he stood awkwardly until she released him.

"Hey, Camelia. I already talked to my mom. She told me you were coming."

He stood apart from her, his head down, his voice—a man's voice—barely audible. If Camelia had seen him pass her by on the street, she would have been struck by how familiar he seemed; he looked like Chris must have at sixteen, only with Melanie's thick, dark curls wreathing the sharp angles of his face. The young boy she used to watch rush in and out of the Sullivan house a few years ago lurked under those curls in a haze of masked emotions.

"Great, good, the phones are working then?" Of course they were aware of her pending arrival. Her heart raced.

"Yeah. Don't worry, she already chewed me out big-time, so you're off the hook." He grinned and gestured languidly toward the path. "There's a room for you, and she said to stay and have a great time. You can eat at the restaurant for free," he added and started walking.

His ambivalence disarmed her; she hurried to keep up.

"Thank you, Nico. Thanks for meeting me and letting me know. Luis told me when I got to Oaxaca that you were here with your dad, so I didn't think it was quite a crisis situation by then. So you're doing OK?"

He shrugged. She tried to figure out how a sixteen-year-old kid might make his way from Santa Fe to this far coastline of Mexico without his mother knowing but was distracted by the lack of a marked pathway through the undergrowth. She saw nothing but palms and the now ubiquitous hibiscus and bougainvillea.

"I don't mean to be rude, but I know you have a hotel hidden in here somewhere." She tried to laugh. A tight metal band of anxiety had begun to wrap itself around her forehead; the taxi driver's words about Señor Chris itched under the surface.

"Here ya go," Nico said, pushing away branches swollen with blossoms and pointing out a narrow brick path hidden in the undergrowth.

Within minutes, a small cluster of buildings appeared, each with a pitched red metal roof and walls mostly of wood slats and screens. She counted a half dozen such casitas tucked into the overgrown hillside as though they were part of the foliage. Another little building, perhaps the hotel's office or maybe a gift shop, sported white dresses awash in brightly colored embroidery hanging in the doorway; they swung gently in the breeze. Peering down the winding path, she spotted a small swimming pool lined in turquoise tiles; a handful of tables were set for dining in a walled-in courtyard behind the pool. From her vantage point on the secluded path, she could see the small restaurant overlooking the beach and the limitless ocean beyond.

She sucked in her breath at the sight, feeling the same kind of inner cleaving she always experienced when she drove north out of Santa Fe just past the opera house, around a curve in the highway and into the vast moonscape of the high desert. The tightness around her forehead suddenly loosened, and her vision cleared. To know the horizon was out there, even if she couldn't see it at the moment in this dense, overripe hothouse of a pathway, was enough. She was a desert rat after all; she needed that limitless vision, those endless possibilities, in front of her. The ocean would most certainly do. Her shoulders finally relaxed.

"Yours is the last one on the path before the construction zone." They wound their way through the heavy branches and overhanging palm fronds past a couple of casitas where she saw the others from the plane letting themselves in. He seemed ready to bolt in the opposite direction.

"What else are you building?" Camelia surveyed the small concrete pads next to her room. Several rods of rebar stuck up out of the cement like an industrial forest. "Are you guys expanding?"

"You'll have to ask my dad," Nico said, already heading back along the path toward the pool.

"Wait a minute, Nico. Where is he? Where are you going?"

"I don't know where he is." Nico tossed the comment over his shoulder. After a beat, he added, "I'll see you around" and disappeared into the jungle.

Camelia stood at the doorway of the tiny cottage shadowed under a massive hibiscus, feeling foolish and alone. The humid sunshine, scented with tropical flowers, the sea, and cook fires from what appeared to be a small village down the coastline reminded her just how far away she was from the messy Santa Fe winter and her mess of a marriage. The warm air grazed her skin like silk. A deep calm unexpectedly settled over her, a peace she had not known in several days, if not weeks. The sudden sensations of timelessness and solitude, so disconnected from her everyday life, stilled her.

She found the key in the lock of the simple screen door: its sturdy metal frame squeaked on rusty hinges. Dropping her duffle on the floor, she pulled a white cotton curtain over the doorway, arranged the mosquito net that hung canopy-like over the bed, fluffed the pillow, and fell into a dreamless sleep.

"It's boring. There's nothing to do there." Nico scooped up more guacamole on a chip. "School sucks, it's so stupid, it's such a waste of time. Who cares who was president a hundred years ago? Why does it matter how to factor algorithms? It's not like I'm going to go work up at the lab in Los Alamos. It's totally irrelevant."

"Yeah, but Nico, every kid everywhere thinks that; it's sort of like your job as a teenager to think that." Camelia scraped up the last bits of grilled fish and tomatoes from her plate with the rest of her corn tortilla. "Running away, scaring your mom to death, you know, that's really not cool, and it doesn't help the situation at all."

"She just pissed me off. She's always bugging me, she like never leaves me alone," he said. "'Nico, build me a fire. Nico, go out and jump start the car. Nico, shovel the walk. Nico, wash your dishes.' God, it sucks. And when my dad is there, she like never gives him a break to just sit back and like chill. No, it's like, 'The *canales* are leaking, the brakes are shot, the principal called,' rag rag rag. God, no wonder he's never around." His dark eyes flashed, and color rose in his cheeks.

It was after nine, and few diners were left in the small dining room. She had slept through the sunset, finally making her way to the restaurant in twilight. Open to the elements, with only a half wall running its perimeter, one corner tucked under *latillas* for shade, the softly lit room felt like the rustic front porch of a secluded estate. Only the presence of Nico, sitting with her at the bar with a Coke and several near-empty plates, served to remind her of Santa Fe and her tenuous reason to be here. Camelia watched the bartender silently drying thick blue glassware at the opposite end of the bar and wondered again where the hell Chris was, anyway. Her heart went out to Melanie.

"Hey, you might want to keep your voice down, Nico," Camelia said. "There's no need for everyone in Dos Palmas to know how you feel about your parents." She pushed the basket of tortilla chips over to him, and he immediately reached for a handful.

"Fuck it, it's not like they don't already know." His voice was still harsh, but he lowered the volume considerably. Camelia felt like an imposter, trying to counsel this angry young man. What would he do when she told him Melanie expected her to bring him back with her? She could easily imagine him flinging the plates to the floor and stomping off. But when he covertly swiped at an unbidden tear, she saw that little kid she used to watch throwing stones at the ravens in Melanie's front yard. Sometimes he would catch lizards in his bare hands, then carefully place them on the front of his shirt and walk around the house, the frozen, clinging thing a proudly worn badge. Rayne, a year or so younger than her brother, would linger nearby, silent.

"You know, Nico, when I got here I thought, my God, this place is beautiful, how could anyone have problems in a place like this? And I used to think the same thing about Santa Fe. I always loved it, and there are so many things that I still love about it today. But it also annoys me—a lot—and I thought, yesterday, what if I were to just leave Santa Fe for good? Just not go back, just, you know, forget about it all and start over someplace else. Maybe your mom and dad would give me a job right here at the hotel, and I could have a simple life on the beach, the kind they dreamed of when they built this place."

She thought about her list scrawled on an old paper bag, and the way her senses were so attached to Santa Fe.

"And then I wondered, well, what would I miss if I left Santa Fe for good?" She stirred the melting ice cubes at the bottom of her Coke with a straw. "And a whole bunch of things came to my mind that I didn't realize were even on my radar, you know? And yet, there they were, sparkling like little jewels in all the dirt and the crap and the things that make me want to run from it all, too."

He looked at her, just a hint of expectation on his face. "Yeah, like what?" A changeling, he had morphed again from that little boy back into a young man, impatient and cocky.

"Well, for starters, there's the food. You know, you can't find real green chile any place but there."

"Yo, Nico, your dad around?" A man with tousled sun-whitened hair and a honeyed tan, a cigarette between his lips, strolled up to the bar. The bartender put a small glass in front of him without a word and filled it from a bottle with no label he had pulled out from under the bar. The man sipped the clear liquid and nodded at her with a smile. His eyes reflected his T-shirt, the blue of the glass, the blue of a Santa Fe sky. She felt a thin line of sweat rise against the skin between her shoulder blades.

"Hey, bro!" Nico said, exchanging one of those purely male thumb-gripping handshakes with the man. "He's not around, dude. I don't know where the fuck he is, but I guess I'll see him sooner or later, since I'm staying in his casita."

"No problemo, I'll catch up with him tomorrow. Who's your friend?" He raised his chin at Camelia. An unfamiliar cadence wrapped and curved around his words.

"Oh yeah, this is my mom's friend Camelia, from Santa Fe." Nico, dismissive, waved his hand toward her, an awkward teenager once more.

"Eric Steadman."

She could smell the woody, mineral cactus in his drink; she could feel her heart beat in her eardrums. She smiled at him.

"Hey, Eric used to live in Santa Fe too, didn't you?" Nico said, reaching over the bar and helping himself to the soda gun.

Eric squinted and looked away; he finished his drink and set the heavy glass on the bar with a sharp clang. "Yep, that's so, my young friend, I did indeed." He signaled the bartender for another, reached into his pocket, and tossed a few bills on the bar.

"Yeah, we were just talking about all the things we actually like about Santa Fe, right, Camelia? Green chile tops the list." Nico laughed.

The bead of sweat slid down her spine. Camelia waved to the bartender.

"*¿Sí, señorita?*"

"Ummm, a margarita, *por favor?*" she asked.

"Oh, you should try some mezcal, Camelia," Nico said, shaking his head at the bartender. "My dad loves it. Eric. Everybody around here drinks it. They make it out there in the hills, all over Oaxaca. Like moonshine almost. It's pretty awesome, better than tequila for sure." He sipped at his Coke with a knowing smile. Eric stubbed out his cigarette, watching her.

"Oh yes, I know about the mezcal." She hesitated. Hammock dreams, sleepwalking, mysterious thunderstorms. Claire used to talk about the magic of Mexico, but perhaps she really meant the mezcal. "My friend Luis in Oaxaca called it '*la medicina*.'"

The bartender nodded and pulled the bottle out from under the counter again. He filled Eric's glass and one for her, squeezing half a *limón* into the drink with a little handheld press, just like Luis had done. And like Luis, before releasing the glass to her, he too instructed her only to sip it. "Don't shoot," he said. "*La medicina, es verdad.*"

"When in Rome," she responded, holding the glass up toward her companions before taking a small sip. The rustic liquor tasted like the spiky grasses of Luis's yard, scratchy on her wrists; this morning was a lifetime ago. A whiff of ocean air moved gently through the darkened restaurant; candles sparkled on the tables.

"What about Fiesta, how crazy is that, burning up that giant puppet while a huge mob chants, 'Burn him, burn him!'" Nico had returned to Santa Fe, his laughter lighting up his eyes and filling the quiet room. "Oh my God, that is so bizarre when you think about it. I'm pretty sure they don't do that in other places."

She sipped again, feeling a now-familiar warmth work its way through her. The desolate dream of the coyote she had on the airplane came back to her, but she knew the real Canyon Road was lush with flowery loveliness in summer and had a still beauty in December. Even though she had skipped the traditional evening walk last year, she easily conjured the sight of the snow falling on Canyon Road on Christmas Eve, the garden walls and rooftops of the low adobe homes lined with paper bags, little candles nestled inside on piles of sand and lit up like a chain of diamonds sparkling on black velvet.

"I always liked the way Santa Fe smelled." Eric lit another cigarette. "Any season, there was always something in the air that smelled good. I thought they should try to bottle it." His voice, low and languid, rolled toward her from miles away: concrete and skyscrapers, dark rooms, jazz.

"Hey, how about this—the fireworks at the racetrack on the Fourth of July?" Nico said. "You could just park anywhere on that mesa over there by La Cienega and watch. And the rodeo, my dad took me to the rodeo once when I was a kid. It was really cool."

"Well, what about driving up the High Road to Taos, did you ever do that?" she asked him, their banter light, their smiles easy now. Oh, she was so pleased; she couldn't wait to call Melanie. She was sure she would have no trouble hanging out for a few days and then bringing Nico back with her. Out of the corner of her eye, she saw the bartender refill Eric's glass yet again and reach toward hers. "Taos is, you know, Taos. And the drive up there through all the little *norteño* villages is kind of cool."

"The Taos gorge, that place is awesome," Nico agreed. "And how about that restaurant on the way there that's right on the Rio Grande, and you can get a raft there and go down the river . . ."

"Yes," Eric piped in. "Under the cottonwood trees; they must be a hundred years old. I know the place, it's like a little brewery, right? They put chile in the beer. And there's an Elvis museum in one of those little adobe houses nearby, ever go there?" She laughed and sipped her drink and watched as Nico dipped his finger into a few drops of mezcal that had spilled on the bar and put it in his mouth with a smile.

And then she was alone, cradling a bottle in her arms and squinting in the dim lamplight along the brick pathway.

"*Para usted,*" the bartender had said, presenting her with a small bottle of mezcal from a shelf behind him when she rose somewhat unsteadily. "*Para todo mal, mezcal, y para todo bien, también.* Enjoy. A gift, from Señor Chris."

Eric had locked eyes with him for a moment, said good-bye suddenly, and disappeared.

Nico had given her a sloppy hug, saying he'd maybe see her on the beach tomorrow.

She tried to remember which of the several pathways in front of her led to her screened-in room. She was sure that having the bottle shatter at her feet would make a very bad impression.

Camelia dreamed of roosters loudly greeting the sun and the faint strains of a brass marching band wafting down the hillside from somewhere above the coastline. Later, pulling open the mosquito netting, she stretched her limbs and padded across the cool tile floor to splash water on her face. From the bathroom window, she took in the view, a sight that again quickened her heart with its wide-open horizon. Perhaps she should just throw on some clothes and go for a walk, today being the first day of the rest of her life and all that.

That first night at Luis's, when she had finally looked in her duffle bag, all she found was denim, denim, and more denim, the uniform of the Southwest. One bright sundress was wadded up underneath everything else; she only wore it when she was sure she wanted to attract attention, which was rare of late. Yesterday, she had hung it up in the tiny closet with the rest of her things and wondered if she'd have the nerve to wear it here. Fingering the dress now, she settled instead on a loose pair of Levi's cut off at the calf and a wrinkled white T-shirt.

Five minutes later, she was down on the beach, clutching her sandals in one hand and steadying her straw hat, the dried bougainvillea blossoms still strung around its crown, with the other. Her orange toenails flashed in the sand. She looked behind her and could see, up on the hillside, the room she had just left. Ahead of her, the coastline curved in a crescent, making for a peaceful bay.

Mexican families with young children were settling in for the morning.

What do I want to do: today, tomorrow, forever? She repeated it to herself like a mantra, keeping time with her steady stride across the beach. The past year, she thought she had finally gotten herself on track to where she was supposed to go, but the whole thing derailed. She couldn't say the crash came without warning. And now, she was tired of wallowing in the wreckage. Luis was right; don't spend your life doing what you don't want to do. The sun was hot on her back, and her legs tingled from the unexpected activity.

"Camelia?"

She turned to see Chris several yards away, slowing from a jog to a brisk walk once he had her attention. His retro tropical print shirt was open over loose khaki pants, his short hair askew. He looked as though he had been sleeping on the beach, although she was sure that wasn't so.

"Hey, glad I caught you." He stopped to catch his breath, resting his hands on his knees before giving her a brief hug. "So you made it in one piece. Helluva trip, isn't it, all those flights. I wish I had known what Melanie was up to, I could have saved you the effort. Not that you aren't of course welcome to have a nice little vacation anyway—always great to see you—but everything's fine. Nico's squared away; it's all good."

He spoke so fast Camelia couldn't tell if he was truly nervous or just caught off guard. He was running his hands through his hair and looking out at the ocean as though he were waiting for something to appear on the horizon. She started to explain, but Chris talked over her, making sudden exclamations about the beautiful weather and how great, again, it was to see her.

"Hey, I have an idea—we're halfway there anyway–let's go get some coffee. Have you had breakfast yet? It's actually almost lunchtime, I think. Let's go get something to eat," he said loudly, steering her along with a hand on her elbow. "So what do you think of the place? You've never been here, have you? Isn't it gorgeous? Can't you tell why we love it so much here?"

"Yes, it's just great. My room is really nice. It's very cozy; thank you so much. And about Nico," she started again.

"Oh, good, I'm glad you like it. Sorry about the construction zone. I know it's not very pretty, but I can assure you, you have the utmost in privacy, considering construction has been stalled since last month. A minor labor disagreement, nothing to worry about, just business as usual in beautiful Dos Palmas."

"Oh, that. So are you guys expanding?" She flicked her hair out of her face and fiddled with the brim of her hat. Now she was the one feeling nervous. So much for Nico, or Melanie, for that matter. She thought of her friend, drunk and crying in the cold February dusk outside Casa Abuelita, demanding Camelia go to Mexico first thing in the morning.

"The truth is, Camelia, although I—Melanie and I—love Dos Palmas very much just as it is, there is a very real possibility that it is poised on the brink of becoming a bona fide resort, and I can't say we're very happy about it."

"You mean like Acapulco?" She eyed the ramshackle nature of a few small beachfront bars. A dozen or so motorboats anchored in the calm bay swayed in the water, just around the curve from the wide beach sparsely populated with young surfers and sunbathers. The boats bore the tarnish of poverty and subsistence, not the glitter of a potential tourism mecca.

"Yes, actually, just like Acapulco." Chris was emphatic. "It gives me a stomachache thinking about it. You just don't know." His eyes grew dark. Camelia had not been to Acapulco, but she had seen enough ads to imagine it. They were probably about as accurate a representation of the real Mexico as the travel magazines were about the real Santa Fe—not that it mattered to people who didn't live there.

"Ah, here we are, one of Dos Palmas's finest dining establishments," Chris said grandly, turning off the beach up a small alleyway and opening the screen door of Mel's Shake Shack for her. A handful of brightly colored chairs and unmatched tables held the signs of a busy morning. Screens all around let in the moist sea air, scented with the unmistakable aroma of coffee. Eric, in a pale chambray shirt, tails out over a pair of baggy Guatemalan shorts, stood behind a low counter and lit a cigarette. He waved when they entered.

Chris and Camelia settled at a table in front, where they could see the beach. "Eric pulls a great espresso, by the way. I highly recommend it," Chris said. "Actually, he's from Santa Fe, too, by way of, where, London? Eric, this is a friend of mine and Melanie's, Camelia Delmonico."

"Small world," Eric said, a smile curling around his cigarette. "Coffee? Latte? Juice?"

"Oh, coffee, sure; maybe some water too?" she said after a moment. She had not expected to feel something open up deep inside her, something soft and wide, that rippled and flowed like a river in an underground cavern.

"Yep, he couldn't hack the pace of the big city, hey, *hermano?*" Chris said. The men laughed, and Eric turned to the cooler for a couple of bottles of water. Camelia gazed out at the beach in front of her, her throat dry as a hot desert wind.

Chris put down his coffee mug and pushed his plate toward the edge of the little table. He seemed obsessed with local politics and the struggles of the small business owners who were his neighbors, and he had chatted amiably about the hotel, about the beach, about the village near by, but not a word about his family or Santa Fe. Camelia picked at the last pieces of melon from what had been a sizable fruit salad and dipped them in the remains of some fresh yogurt in a small plastic bowl.

Finally relaxed, she let his monologue take over while she ate. She watched Eric as he made espresso and served up fruit bowls and sweet rolls to an endless parade of young people, most of whom took their food to the beach. He worked in concert with a jovial, heavy-set Mexican woman who bustled around the small place with an owner's pride. Perhaps his wife, she wondered idly, her eyes following the pair as they joked good-naturedly in both Spanish and English with each other and the steady stream of customers.

"So, Camelia, what's the story with you and Michael?" Chris said, changing the tenor of the conversation without warning. "I hear things are not going so well." He looked up toward Eric at the counter and pointed at his coffee cup for a refill.

"Well, that's one way to put it."

"Thanks, old man; great lunch," Chris said as Eric poured them both more coffee and stacked up their empty plates with his free hand. She waited to speak until he stepped away from the table.

"Actually, he left, and to be honest, Chris, I'm not really sure if he's coming back or if he moved back into his own apartment for good," she said quietly. Her eyes filled unexpectedly, and she felt singularly exposed. Everyone in the small café was surely looking at her. He kept his own apartment after you got married? What were you thinking? She had said the same things to herself innumerable times over the last six months.

Chris ran his palm over the stubble on his chin and down his throat. A thin strand of robin's-egg-blue turquoise beads encircled his sun-brown neck. Camelia looked away, an uncomfortable heat rising within her as his hand idly caressed the stones.

"Well, there really isn't anything else to say, is there?" he said finally. "When a guy doesn't want to be somewhere, he lets you know. It's no mystery. Guys are pretty easy to read, actually. We're not very complicated creatures. Eat. Sleep. Drink. Sex. There's not that much more to it, when you think about it." He grinned, though his eyes seemed sad, and Camelia could see Nico in his face as he pushed his chair out from the table and stood.

"Later, *hermano*," he called to Eric, who was washing a sink full of dishes, and waited for Camelia to go out the door first. She fumbled with her hat and tried to collect her thoughts as they stepped back out on the beach.

"Thanks again for coming down here to check on Nico," Chris said, his voice low and focused even though his eyes swept the beach ahead of them. "Melanie and I, we're working things out. It's not such a big deal. I'm sorry she overreacted and got you involved. If she'd waited another hour, I could have told her so myself. The phones suck, and it's a big problem here, really compromises business—you can imagine." He started walking, his face a mask. She hurried alongside him, certain that he required nothing of her in this moment except her silence.

"So look, I'll be sure Nico goes back with you. He can't stay here, that's for sure. There's school, and, you know, I can't keep track of him down here. There's too much going on that . . . well, anyway, thanks, Camelia, but really, don't worry about it. I got it covered."

She fine-tuned her attention on the sound of the sea at her side as they headed back to the hotel.

"Hey, day after tomorrow is Carnaval." His voice was again full, almost jovial. "Tuesday, right? I'll pick you up at your room in the morning, early. I'm taking a few of the guests up into the mountains, where there are several little villages, for some local color." He waved his arm away from the expanse of ocean and toward the rugged topography in the distance.

"Sure, that sounds like fun." She forced a smile.

"Listen, Camelia, I have some people I need to see up here." He gestured toward the road that ran parallel to the beach before threading its way inland. A young woman in a tiny bathing suit, a silky orange *pareo* wrapped around her slender waist, perched on a low adobe wall at the edge of the sand. She stood and waved when she saw Chris; he nodded back.

"Enjoy yourself, and don't forget to wear sunscreen; we have some at the gift shop. I'll see you around, Tuesday morning for sure. You need anything, just ask Emiliana at the front office, and she'll take care of you." He turned to face her for a moment even as he continued walking away. "And don't worry about anything. Really, it's not that complicated."

Nope, not complicated at all, she thought as she walked back up the brick path to her little room. It was so obvious, Melanie must know; she had to at least have an idea about it. Maybe that was why she insisted Camelia come here now, to confirm what she suspected.

She flung her hat on the chest of drawers and sat on the bed, flopping back to stare at the ceiling. Men. They'll tell you everything you need to know about them in the first five minutes, Claire had said once. If you don't listen, whose fault is that? *I'm really busy trying to build my career, and, you know, my childhood was basically miserable, and I'm not really all that interested in the whole family thing*—wasn't that what Michael had told her on their very first date? She felt heat start to collect in her chest, a firestorm gathering over her heart. She eyed the bottle of mezcal on the end table.

"Well, I can sit in here and cry my head off, or I can go sit by the pool, get a tan, and have a nice, cold drink. Which one do I think I want to do?" she said aloud to the empty room. The cotton curtains wavered in the sea breeze.

8 *Maybe He Just Didn't Care*

Ah, paradise. The familiar words rang out in Eric's head the next morning just as they had almost every morning for the last three years. He winced at the smell of rotting fruit and urine that mingled with the scent of the early morning fires of his neighbors, who were heating up breakfast in the alley. Yes, here it is: the easy life, the beach life, the life every corporate middle manager dreams of escaping to. He stepped over the fresh piles of dog shit, the split coconuts, the downed palm fronds drying in the already hot sun around the front door of Mel's Shake Shack. The lock, replaced for the third or fourth time not long ago, was already gritty with sand and salt air. Must everything rot?

It was just past six. He lit a cigarette and turned on the coffeepot, opened the latches on the three wooden shutters covering the screened windows facing the Pacific, then opened up the side panels as well, even though he knew smoke from the alley would waft inside. His own handmade wooden tables, with their handful of mismatched chairs collected from around the village, were shiny from the moist air and dotted with crumbs. They would all need to be wiped down, he noted, wondering if he had just not bothered to do it yesterday or if it had been perhaps several days since he had attended to them. "Who knows, who cares," he muttered out loud and pulled several green-speckled oranges from a tall basket under the counter in preparation for his morning juicing routine.

A dangerous realization had slowly begun creeping into Eric's consciousness the last few months. Here he was, with a simple bungalow in a remote tropical fishing village and a little business on the beach, just a stone's throw from the sea. No pressures, no deadlines. He didn't even have to wear shoes. His fortieth birthday had quietly come and gone some time ago, and he could still boast to anyone that he lived like some university kid on permanent vacation. And yet all he saw anymore was shit. Everywhere, shit. What the fuck was wrong with him.

He knew he wasn't the only one for whom life in tiny Dos Palmas had begun to chafe. Just yesterday, Eric had noted the new wrinkles in the corners of Chris' eyes, felt a vague cloud of dissatisfaction swirl about him as he was chatting up his pretty friend from Santa Fe over lunch.

When Eric had first arrived at the beach with nothing but his tools in the back of his pickup truck, Chris was the first person he'd met. Over shots of mezcal at the bar of the Hotel Paloma Blanca, he gratefully accepted Chris's offer of a small room while he got himself squared away in exchange for his carpentry skills on projects around the hotel. It was a modest place, but he could tell Chris had big plans. Soon enough, Chris had gotten him set up at Mel's, abandoned already by more than one starry-eyed gringo who couldn't hack the way things got done—or not—here. "The more things for tourists here, the better," Chris had said, helping him move in the new espresso machine. The shake shack had been Melanie's idea, back when they first started building the Paloma Blanca; he never bothered to take the old sign down, didn't care when tourists called him Mel.

Melanie used to sit on the front porch of their casita and write in a notebook on her lap while their kids, Nico and Rayne, roamed the beach or the village, went out on the fishing boats, or hung around with him, drinking smoothies. Eric had taught Nico, then only thirteen or fourteen, a few rudimentary wood carving techniques and even supervised the making of a crude wooden table before the boy suddenly became restless and evasive.

Shortly after that, the whole family seemed to have just packed up and move away. He couldn't remember the last time he saw Melanie or the kids at the beach. Once in a while he'd have a drink with Antonio, their Mexican business partner, who apparently spent most of his time in Mexico City lobbying various government officials and massaging regulations. He told Eric he'd come down to the beach to keep an eye on things at the Paloma Blanca, but he never stayed long. Then one night, there was Chris pouring shots of tequila at the hotel bar for a bunch of surfers, and now he seemed once again like a permanent fixture in Dos Palmas. Bloody hell, so much coming and going around here, he didn't try to keep it all straight.

An old pickup truck blasted its way down the alley, pausing for a moment at his threshold to release its passenger. "*¿Qué tal?*" he called out to Esperanza, reaching over to open the door for her, then turning back to his oranges. She carried an unwieldy basket filled with small loaves of bread, neatly covered with a multicolored cloth one of her six sisters had woven. Eric hollered, "*¡Adios!*" to her husband, Miguel, who waved out the truck window as he rattled away.

"*Buen día,*" she huffed, setting down the basket and heading behind the counter.

"Work, work, work, that's all life is about." Ignoring Esperanza's greeting, Eric spoke more to himself than to her as he looked out the side windows at several children who suddenly appeared, playing noisily in the alley. Sleepy but not complaining, they clustered around the fires for a hot breakfast of fresh tortillas and just-caught fish before starting a busy day working on the beach.

"You're two years old and still wearing a grimy old nappy, and they throw you out on the beach to the tourists to peddle some pathetic little baggie of oversalted *cacahuates*," he said, gesturing out the window. "You grow up, and if you're not careful, you might find yourself spending your mornings slicing oranges for surfers and praying you don't cut your thumb off."

Esperanza turned off the faucet where she had been washing her hands, letting the suds grow like mittens. A black braid thick as rope hung down her back, shiny and dark against her white embroidered *huipil*.

"And how are we this beautiful morning?" Her eyes narrowed at him, and her needling tone easily penetrated her heavy accent. When she first came to Mel's to work for Eric, she asked him to teach her English in exchange for Spanish lessons; today few conversations within earshot escaped her. Eric's Spanish, on the other hand, remained limited, burdened under the British inflection he hadn't been able to shake.

"Your head, it is hurting this morning?"

"I know, I know, I complain about the very idea of work every morning. Never mind, I don't mean it, don't listen to me," Eric said, waving her away.

"Oh, *sí*, you say that every morning, too. But you don't mean that either." Esperanza laughed, a rich, easy, rolling sound that rose from her center and filled the tiny restaurant. A mother of five and not yet out of her twenties, Esperanza was Eric's only employee. He called her his chief cook and bottle washer in English, *señora* when the local men came in, and *mi salvadora* when he thanked her for paying herself out of the cash register every afternoon.

His complaining sounded just like the spoiled Eurotrash he had left behind in New York years ago, and he hated it. He knew if it wasn't for work, he'd be dead or close to it, strung out in some anonymous backstreet anywhere in the world, a bottle broken over his head, a needle stuck in his arm. The meditative rhythm of slicing the oranges and putting them in the press one half at a time kept his hands steady. By the time he put his first pitcher of juice in the refrigerator, he could pour a cup of coffee without spilling it. He lit a cigarette and filled a second pitcher with juice, debating and finally deciding against spiking a glass for himself from the bottle of vodka tucked in the back of the freezer.

Instead, he watched as Esperanza unloaded the loaves of sweet bread, baked in the middle of the night and some of them still warm, onto a stack of handmade clay plates. Their earthy fragrance rose up around him. She concentrated on pulling plastic wrap off a large roll mounted under the counter and wrapping each plate the way he had shown her. Tomorrow, if there were any left, they would still be soft as down beneath their crunchy crusts, their flavor as sunny and mellow as the day itself.

"And yes, I do have a headache, Señora Mind Reader," he said, rummaging around in the drawer under the cash register for the ibuprofen. The pounding in his head had begun with a slow rumble but was now starting to kick in with greater force. "What do you think, Esperanza? Perhaps it was that last bucket of pulque late last night making my head feel like a split melon this morning? Thick, nasty stuff, that."

"What do I think? I think you find a good woman and stay home at night, not sit in the bars drinking all the time," she said, dismissing his misery with a wave of her hand.

"You know, if I didn't have to open this joint so early in the day in order to keep you employed, I could stay in bed for a few extra hours. Then I could stay out all night, and I wouldn't have such a hard time getting going in the morning." He leaned on the counter and smoked as she deftly cut fruit for the smoothies, filled coffee filters with ground coffee, poured water into the steam chamber for the lattes that would soon be ordered.

"Oh, *sí*, of course, and then what would you do with yourself?"

"Hey, I don't have to open up at all, *¿tu sabes?*" he said with a laugh. There were plenty of mornings when he woke up just long enough to say, "Fuck it, I'm staying home." But here he was, just the same. This is what I do, he would say aloud as he roused himself up against even a hurricane-force hangover. Better that I have someplace to be at dawn than no place to be all day except on the beach or in the bar. Otherwise, I would never get up. Or maybe I would never go to bed.

Esperanza continued to bustle about. Eric knew the idea of staying in bed for a few extra hours was as foreign to her as the espresso machine on the counter, which she at first refused to learn how to operate. Today, of course, she was a casually perfect barista, but that's what you get when you want to rise out of bed every morning and you want to go to work. Such sturdy arms, he thought, such a sturdy soul. Such a full life, making do with so little. How can it be fair when, truly, I have so much more and yet so much less than she?

They worked quickly, knowing the first customers would be showing up shortly. Esperanza worked at Mel's every day until two, when Miguel roared down the alley again in his fall-apart pickup, a tangle of children squealing from the truck bed, to collect her. Twice a week, he dropped off a couple sacks of oranges and a carton of fruit as well. Eric would stay another hour or so, doling out smoothies and rolls on his own, then lock the door and walk down the beach to his casita. As he had every day since he had come here, he would nap for a few hours in the hammock, handwoven by one of Esperanza's relatives and strung between a couple of convenient palm trees. He would take a long walk on the beach in the late afternoon sun, collecting plastic cups and paper napkins and water bottles as he went and dumping them in the few trash cans scattered around the beach. He'd eat dinner at the Paloma Blanca, or perhaps a fish shack over by the bay, before facing the warm, moonless night alone. Alone, that is, until he'd decide to go out for a quick drink.

Trying to find something to distract him from the jackhammer in his head, Eric's thoughts turned again to Chris and his lunch date yesterday. Camelia, that was her name. She had been friendly, even festive, when he met her at the hotel bar the other night with Chris's son, Nico. But yesterday, she ignored him while she tried not to cry, Chris's arm gingerly around her shoulder. Even in her grief she seemed to radiate; perhaps it was just that her pain was so raw, so exposed, he found he could not look away.

Last night, Eric had seen her yet again, sitting alone at a dark table in a corner of the Bar el Dorado. She had a shot glass, a small bottle with no label, and a bowl of cut *limones* on the table in front of her. He watched her from the shadows where he sat with a few men he knew from the village. She, in turn, watched the surfers and the fishermen, and then she disappeared. If she had seen him, she didn't show it. He considered following her, perhaps even offering to walk her back to the hotel, but changed his mind when another round of the local pulque, a sort of crude agave beer that never failed to make him feel regret the next day, appeared on the table.

"So, Esperanza, *mi amiga*, have you seen Chris's friend from Santa Fe at the Paloma Blanca?" he asked casually, lighting another cigarette. Several of Esperanza's sisters worked at the small hotel, on the grounds or in the tiny restaurant, as did her neighbors, her cousins, and many members of Miguel's family. There was no news in Dos Palmas Esperanza wouldn't know, and if it generated from the Paloma Blanca, she'd have learned about it before the tides changed. Eric heard everything from Esperanza, but every time she would start up with a tale of a young woman leaving Chris's casita early in the morning, he would put his hands over his ears.

"Don't tell me; believe me, I don't want to know," he'd always say. Eric had sometimes seen Chris at the local bars, drinking with surfers and other young travelers, mezcal probably drowning any illusions he might have had about discretion. But it was Melanie, after all, who had pushed Chris to give Eric the abandoned restaurant in the first place. It was an inspired idea that probably saved his life; he owed her at least this consideration, even in her absence.

"Oh, *sí, la señorita Camelia, es como una flor blanca*," Esperanza said, just as casually but with a curious eye turned toward him.

"And?"

"Ah, *pobrecita*," she answered, shaking her head. "Her heart, it's broken, like all of Señora Melanie's friends who come from Santa Fe. *Pero* I think she'll get over it."

"Yeah, that's what I thought." He remembered how Chris and Camelia sat ten feet from him so thoroughly engrossed, it was as if he was not there. And something had stirred within Eric, a sensation he had grown quite unaccustomed to. It was not an altogether unpleasant feeling, he noted now, with the advantage of distance, but one that confused him nonetheless. He made careful note of the fact that Esperanza had said Camelia was Melanie's friend. That had to count for something.

"Hey, dude, time to pour some java, man!" The first sleepy surfers began straggling in around seven, awaking from dreams of flying. Unwashed even after days of living in the water, they brought with them the smell of the sea. Salt and sand were encrusted in their hair, coated their skin, flurried off their clothes like fine snow when they moved.

They drank coffee, hot and sweet with lots of milk in it. They craved the fresh-squeezed juice and paid per cup what it cost Eric to buy a whole basketful of oranges. They scarfed down Esperanza's sugary breads with butter and jam, spooned yogurt on granola, drank smoothies made from fruit, milk, and honey. Within half an hour, wired on carbs and caffeine, they headed to the water as one and began the daily quest for the transcendence of the perfect wave.

Surfers often came to Dos Palmas for the whole season, and Eric recognized many of them this morning, having seen them several times drinking at one of the two bars in the village. The Punto de Luz and the Bar el Dorado were both funky, undemanding watering holes made lively by the presence of the dreadlocked, tattooed youth. One had an ancient jukebox that only played when it was kicked, so every song had a thumping preamble. The other was filled with the scratchy sounds of a tinny radio struggling to catch the signals over the mountains from Ciudad Oaxaca.

If one of the kids brought in a boombox, the incongruous sound of reggae music would fill the Mexican air. Eric had often seen the villagers, as they were enjoying a cold *cerveza*, narrow their eyes and mumble to each other about the bad element that had taken over their beach, but the surfers remained oblivious. He knew they saw only the surf, sand, and palm trees; they could just as easily be on a beach in Australia or Thailand, rather than the isolated Mexican fishing village of Dos Palmas.

"Now there's a life," Eric said to Esperanza when the last of the surfers pushed an empty cup across a table and headed out the door after his friends. "How much more meaningless and empty and totally pointless could it get?"

"They want to spend the day surfing, that's fine with me," she said over the clatter of the coffee pots in the sink. "They think they walk on water. But if someone should be needed to take their place back home, they can call me. I'm glad to go to college and learn enough to move to Mexico City and get a good job."

"Get a good job?" He smiled. "Are you kidding? You've got the best job in Dos Palmas right here."

"Oh, sí, and thanks to you, *patrón*, I have a babysitter and a big house and I hire a norteamericana to clean it!" She splashed Eric with the sudsy water and bustled out to the front to clear the tables.

Shortly after the surfers left, a few fishermen came in for breakfast. They had missed their early morning run but would make up for it by taking tourists out to a lush inland lagoon later in the day.

"*Chocolate con leche, por favor, señora,*" they each said, ordering her pan dulce to dunk in it. They kept up a steady dialogue about the weather, which had about as much variety as the breakfast they ordered every morning, Eric thought, although he didn't say so. They came in for Esperanza's spiced, foamy chocolate several mornings a week and hung out with Eric at the bars in the evenings. They often bought him drinks and teased him about his tan.

"No matter how long you stay here, no matter how brown your skin gets, *amigo*, you will never be mistaken for a *mexicano* because of that white hair," they'd say. Like his hair, his steely eyes seemed to grow lighter too, yet his skin held the sun fast, like any island baby. He would laugh with them, waving the white palms of his hands and comparing the color of his forearms with theirs.

They tried to sell him *mota* sometimes to smoke but he always refused, preferring instead the slow, clear melancholy of the local spirits. Sometimes they offered him women they knew from the village—not their own sisters or daughters, of course, but women they knew without men. He always declined, as politely as possible so as not to offend, and would even occasionally point between his legs with a grin and a shrug, pretending that maybe it just didn't work anymore or maybe he just didn't care. Which, to be honest, he didn't.

After a small wave of lunch customers, Mel's was quiet again in the early afternoon. Esperanza swept the floor, pushing the sand outside one more time. She collected her day's pay from the cash register, wrapping it carefully in a colorful scrap of handwoven cloth, and hopped into Miguel's waiting truck. Eric stood in the doorway smoking for a moment after she left and watched four sunburned tourists pick their way through the alley. Their jagged urban voices ripped the soft air. Out for a scenic adventure among *la gente* and maybe a cup of fresh juice if they think they can trust it, Eric thought as he flipped the fag into the sand and went back inside to wait for them.

"Oh, look, an espresso machine, thank God!" one of the women cried, removing her dark glasses with a clatter. Most likely she would not have been out of place within the Paloma Blanca's brightly tiled walls, but everything about her was too big for this humble beach—from her wide-brimmed black straw hat to the clunky plastic bangles on her arms and oversized beads around her neck. Even her voice was too large for the small café. Eric could barely let them finish ordering in their mangled Spanish.

"I bet you're from New York," he said with a smile, and he saw the two couples visibly relax. He wanted to walk out the door and into the sea. Instead, he set about making four espressos, a painstakingly slow process that gave them ample time to question him about how he landed in Dos Palmas. It was such an oddly favorite pastime for tourists; Eric had told his story so many times it had become a performance.

"Yeah, I lived in New York years ago. I got lost almost as soon as I got off the bleedin' plane." Hazy memories circled around the edges of an old darkness best left hidden. "Sex, drugs, and rock 'n' roll, right?" The room filled with knowing laughter over the hum of the espresso machine.

"But, you know, eventually I wanted to get out of the city, see something of America besides big buildings and dark nightclubs." As he knew they would, the tourists heartily agreed. He pulled four tiny spoons out from under the counter and placed them on saucers while he waited for the rich coffee to finish dripping. He felt as though he was talking about someone else.

"The further west I got, the better I could breathe. One day I traded my motorcycle for a pickup truck and decided to stay put in the desert for a while. And then, well, did you know that you can drive straight to Dos Palmas from Santa Fe without ever having to turn left or right?" This comment always elicited exclamations of surprise combined with a brief diversion into questions about Santa Fe, and today's audience was no different.

"Ah, but that's a story to save for a rainy day," he said, wrapping up his little act with the distribution of espressos, discussion of Esperanza's baked goods, and directions to a small pizzeria owned by an Italian at the other end of the beach. As he expected, the two couples scribbled their New York addresses on a napkin and urged Eric to visit the next time he found his way north. When they left, he dropped the napkin in a box under the counter stuffed with similar notes, each one a record of a conversation just like today's.

By now, he was tired and ready to call it a day. It was time for siesta, he noted as he washed the espresso cups, or maybe time for something else entirely. His hands swooshed about in the soapy water. If cats have nine lives, how many do people get? Wiping his hands on a towel, yet another item woven by Esperanza's sisters, Eric decided that if he did get to choose another life, he'd better do it soon. This one was beginning to wear thin.

Just as he was about to call it a day, Camelia came hurrying up the alley.

"Oh, you're not closed yet, are you? I was hoping to just get a little roll or something for lunch." She wore a simple black tank bathing suit with a bright pareo wrapped around her waist like a skirt. Its magenta fringe dusted her ankles; dried bougainvillea circled the crown of her straw hat.

He paused only a moment. "Hey, come on in. I've got a few things left over, it's no problem." She had obviously spent the day in the sun and had a pleasing pinkish tan. He wrapped up a couple of Esperanza's panes dulces and put them in a bag, along with a piece of banana bread. "I can make you a smoothie if you like, quick as a New York minute," he said, suddenly wanting to make her stay. She nodded and smiled.

"Look, I'm sorry about just coming in here yesterday morning and losing it completely," she said over the noise of the blender.

"No problemo," he answered, pouring her drink into a plastic cup. He saw her eyes land briefly on the three-by-five card tacked to the doorjamb, advertising AA meetings in English at the local church. "Oh, that . . ." he started, but she was already looking at the array of other cards, notes, and fliers hanging around the door and on the wall, and his voice trailed to a stop.

Oh, but she is lovely, he thought. And he wanted to speak to her, not about Dos Palmas, not about Mel's Shake Shack, but about her. I saw you in the bar, he wanted to say; I saw you looking like the loneliest person in the world. But he didn't. Instead he gave her the smoothie and the bag of food. Waving her money away—"Any friend of Melanie is a friend of mine"—he offered to walk her back to the hotel.

"So how long did you live in Santa Fe, anyway?" she asked as they walked along the shoreline, dodging small children who had dressed themselves in wet sand. "It seems like you must have been here for a while."

"Let's see, I've been here already for what, three years now? Before that, just a few years in Santa Fe; I'm not sure I would really call it home," he said. *Home.* And in that sudden and precise and unexpected moment, he knew he had truly fallen off the edge of the world here in Dos Palmas, and his breath froze in his lungs. He rubbed his eyes and steered Camelia off the beach into the sandy front doorway of the Punto de Luz.

"I think I could use a drink all of a sudden. Will you join me?" he said, looking, not at her face, but at her hands, where a white band of skin on her tanned left ring finger gave away the fact that she had removed her wedding ring perhaps only moments ago.

The empty bar was dark and cool. Eric nodded to Eloy, who was quietly sweeping near the back of the room; he shrugged and jutted his chin toward the bar. Eric reached behind, helping himself to an unlabeled bottle and a couple of glasses. Walking toward a table, he said, "Let's see, must have been about five years ago, now, all told. I still remember the first thought that came into my mind that day I arrived in New Mexico."

She sat down across from him, her attentive gaze disconcerting. He poured mezcal in each glass and gazed at it before speaking. "I wanted to do something with my hands. I had it in my head that that alone would save me."

"Save you? From what?" she said, squeezing a *limón* from a bowl on the table into her glass. He watched as the juice clouded the liquor, swirling like a sudden storm over the desert.

"From myself." He was surprised with the confessional clarity of his own statement; would she bestow a forgiveness he didn't know he sought? She looked at him over the rim of her glass.

"I grew up on a small farm, actually," he went on, ignoring whatever had begun buzzing around inside him since she had arrived at his door. "I left when I was sixteen, hitched my way to London, and worked there for a while with some punk bands, you know, and next thing I knew, I was in New York."

For a moment he thought he heard the clanking of oversized black bangles and glanced over his shoulder. "I managed to survive that city a bloody long time, but eventually I knew I would die if I didn't put these hands to work again. Once I got to New Mexico, I discovered wood."

His lip curled in a half smile, his eyes locked on the mezcal as he tilted it around in the glass. "Ah, the foolishness of dreams. Youth is bittersweet." Finally, he sipped his drink. *La medicina* indeed.

"We all make mistakes." She shrugged. "You're hardly the first guy who wanted the rock 'n' roll life. At least you managed to get out before it killed you. You should probably consider yourself lucky; not everyone does. Get out, I mean. So what did you do there? I mean, in Santa Fe? Were you a builder? A carpenter?"

She seemed nervous; she spoke fast, faster than he was used to. He wondered what mistakes of her own she might be referring to. "Yeah, I started apprenticing to a woodworker from El Rito, up north. He taught me the basics of furniture making."

Eric had found a particular affinity with wood, and now he realized how much he missed it. The chisels and awls rested in his fingers as though they lived there; his hands were like a lover's when he rubbed in the soft wax finish. Camelia filled his glass and her own; he didn't realize they were already empty. Memories of his life in Santa Fe flooded through him. Crystalline skies and the crisp scent of burning piñon. Listening to the soft sounds of Santa Fe's Spanish radio station and sleeping with his arms around the woman who was having his child. He didn't know then if he loved her, or even if he ever had, but he had loved the roundness of her swelling belly and the life he had a part in creating.

"I was married for a while, and we had a kid, a boy, but, you know, things didn't really go so well." He rubbed a spot on the table. Home. Yes, for about a minute. Shelley didn't want to have the child at first, she didn't want to stay in New Mexico, and she didn't want to be with him. She had pushed him away more often than not, until he moved into the little room at the rear of the house that had become his workshop. A chilled bottle of vodka had kept him and his carving tools company those long, solitary nights.

"I kind of had this fantasy, you know?" Now he couldn't stop himself; a cloud of mezcal wound itself around his tongue, his limbs, his head. "I actually wanted that whole picket-fence thing. Instead, I found myself wandering into the hospital in a vodka haze in the middle of the night and demanding a vasectomy."

He laughed darkly and almost spilled the bottle as he poured another shot. The vodka, the sharp tools, the many nights he sat in his workshop contemplating doing the job himself. What did he know about being a father, a husband?

"They refused, of course. That time, anyway."

Camelia was silent. Now he knew he should stop talking, but he seemed to have forgotten how.

"Santa Fe. It's ancient, that place. Rooted. It holds you. And it was roots that I wanted; I wanted to know I was home." He lit a cigarette. Domestic bliss: what a joke. He had nightmares of being carried by strong brown arms to the top of a handmade mountain, his body a gift to the all-devouring fire. And he would welcome the fire.

"And then, you know, everything changed," he murmured, now lost, still lost. "Solid ground became much less stable."

"Oh, I know how that is." Her voice, raw from the alcohol, surprised him; he had forgotten her. She reached for the bag of food. "What happened? How'd you wind up here?"

He blinked; it took him a moment to remember. "It was the craziest thing. I took this set of wooden doors to a new house north of town. The owner of the house, a Hollywood director, was in L.A., so the gardener, a local dude, you know, he let me in. He helped me install the doors, and then he offered me a joint. So we sit on this moss-rock wall to smoke, and we're laughing about the ridiculous proportions of the house—oh, you should have seen it, it was just enormous—when suddenly he gets this crazy look in his eye. 'It's still our town, you know, even though they think it's theirs now,' he says, and I'm thinking, oh no, here we go."

Eric could still see the young Hispanic man toying with the cigarette lighter in his hand, flicking it into flame over and over again, then aiming the flame at the house and breaking into a wild laughter that raised the hairs on Eric's arms.

"So I just kind of laughed with him and headed home. And then when I got to my street, I passed it. I thought, I must be buzzed or something because I just missed my turn, but you know, I didn't stop or turn around. I just kept going. And then I was on the highway. And then I was passing Albuquerque. It wasn't until I was all the way down in Las Cruces that I realized I wasn't going back."

"Jesus. Talk about your disappearing acts," Camelia said. "Now, me, I figured I had to go back. It wouldn't even occur to me to buy a one-way ticket."

Eric had forgotten how tired he was while he was talking, but now he felt exhausted. He had never told anyone except Chris why he left Santa Fe, and here he had just spilled it all to a stranger as though she were holding a lit fag to his eyeball.

She was talking now about Santa Fe and her husband; what a yob that guy was, though no worse than himself, he was sure. He knew he should drag himself out of the bar and head home before he drank any more or said any more or looked into her sad, sorry eyes anymore, but he couldn't move. He was anchored to the chair, his whole life and everything he would ever count on again depending on him staying in the Punto de Luz for just a little while longer. I will leave when she does, he decided. That way, I know I will not have overstayed my welcome.

". . . so when Melanie said, 'No, *you* go to Dos Palmas,' I thought, Why not?" she was saying as she squeezed another *limón* into her glass.

The bag of food was torn and empty; crumbs and crusts littered the table along with lime rinds, cigarette ashes, and sticky rings left from the bottoms of countless glasses before theirs. He had long ago lost track of how much they were drinking. Eric watched her mouth as she spoke, saw the white teeth behind tender lips, wondered if she would taste like mezcal or perhaps more like lime.

"I mean, it was really getting laughable, how far apart we had gotten. We hardly had sex anymore. Most of his stuff was still at his own apartment. We had become two strangers, still hanging onto each other for God knows what, some kind of fucked-up security or something. And I knew he wouldn't have the courage to tell me it was over. He would just wait it out, drawing into himself like a turtle, or an ostrich, maybe, waiting until the end of the world or until I officially broke up with him, whichever came first," she said. "Facing reality isn't the easiest thing in the world to do, but I think the alternative is worse, don't you?"

Clumsy now, her eyelids heavy, she helped herself to a cigarette from his pack on the table. Eric wondered suddenly if Shelley had filed a missing person report. Had she looked for him? More than likely, she would have been relieved he was gone and gotten on with her life. He wondered where they lived, if they had stayed in the same house or perhaps had even moved away from Santa Fe. Camelia's knee brushed against his under the table.

"When I first got here, a couple days ago, I thought about just staying here and never leaving," she said, her words sliding, her eyes moist. He lit the cigarette for her and one for himself. "Women disappear from Santa Fe all the time. I could just start over, with one suitcase. I'd do anything rather than have to go back there and clean up the wreckage."

Eric looked at his hands on the dirty table. He closed his eyes; he swayed like a palm in the wind. Before he could talk himself out of the moment of sudden clarity he felt, he corked the mezcal bottle and called to Eloy, *"¡Dos cafés, por favor!"*

"Listen. I know it sounds appealing. I did it, remember? Who was just talking about reality, babe? The reality is, time doesn't stop. One day you wake up, and you wonder where you've been all this time." His voice was low and intense, and he listened to his own words as though they were a code he had finally broken.

"You put not only your past but your future behind you. You close your heart because the pain is unbearable. You drink yourself into darkness every night. You forget what pleasure is, and what desire is, and you won't feel you deserve it when it knocks at your door." He watched her eyes fill with tears.

"Will he miss you? Will he wonder where you are? Have you called him?"

She got up unsteadily and went to the bar, asked Eloy where the *baño* was, and made her way around the corner. Eric knew he could get up and leave while she was gone and pretend that her visit had not changed him. He knew that it would take more mezcal than ever to help him sleep if he did.

9 Carnaval

Camelia dragged herself out from under the mosquito netting and peered, gritty-eyed, out the screen door, a bedsheet hastily wrapped around her naked body. Chris, neatly dressed this morning in khaki shorts and a white Oxford shirt with rolled sleeves, smiled brightly in the early morning sun. He continued to drum on the metal doorframe.

"We're going up the mountain for Carnaval, remember? Be in front at nine if you want to go." His manner was brisk, professional. Today, she was just another guest at the hotel, albeit one who got personal delivery of both a cup of chocolate con leche and a bottle of ibuprofen. He disappeared into the foliage before she could respond.

Oh, to climb back into her cave and sleep for a thousand years. Last night was a blur. After making their way back toward the hotel in silence, leaving Eric somewhere along the beach, she had slept the rest of the afternoon away. At the moment, she wasn't even sure if she had made it out for dinner. Never mind about what did she *want* to do with her life; what the hell was she doing with it now?

Clanky American voices wafted up the hillside from one of the casitas below. She sucked down the chocolate, hurriedly dressed, and headed down the stone steps. She was the last of a handful of passengers to climb into the hotel van. Chris announced to the little group that he had several stops planned.

"Just so you have some kind of idea of what to expect, Carnaval is a two-day celebration throughout much of our country before the church holiday of Ash Wednesday and the beginning of Lent. And just like Mardi Gras in New Orleans or Carnival in Rio, festivities in many of the indigenous mountain villages around here are what you might think of as a kind of weird combination of ancient tribal ritual and somewhat distorted Catholic rite." He pulled slowly out from the hotel's rugged alley-like entrance and drove on the paved highway for just a short distance before turning onto another road just as crude, hardly more than a trail in threat of being overtaken by jungle growth. Camelia was grateful for the ibuprofen.

"Each village, some of them with no more than two or three extended families whose ancestors were called the Cloud People, has its own fiesta, its own special foods, even its own brass marching band. Yet for Carnaval, their celebrations are all one."

The van, like Luis's Bug, was another Volkswagen relic from the '60s. It labored its way up the mountain, stifling conversation. She was reminded of the rough road Luis drove daily to and from his secluded aerie in Oaxaca. The washboard dirt roads near her own house in Santa Fe ran slick and gooey during the July monsoons, were rutted and icy in the winter, and threw clouds of dust when it was dry. But in some of Santa Fe's wealthier neighborhoods, there was a strong resistance to road maintenance and paving. Privacy, said some. Neglect, said others.

Spent plastic water bottles coated with a layer of fine red dust rattled and slid under the seat and across the floor. Her feet, already swollen in the heat of early day, felt tight in her sandals. From the seat in front of her, the high, flat voice of one of the hotel guests droned on, filling up what little pockets of air blew through the old van as it creaked and groaned.

Keeping a steady watch out the window, Camelia allowed the green and red and brown to form a comforting blur. Chris had handed out pieces of fruit and *pan dulce* when they started off, and now she concentrated on eating.

". . . so we left San Cristóbal at the beginning of January and decided to come to Dos Palmas through February. My Spanish teacher here is just so much better than the one I had in Chiapas," the woman in front of her said.

Chiapas. The word hung in Camelia's mind like the bright, multicolored hammocks hanging from the portals around the resort, waking her momentarily from a slight doze. She rarely paid attention to the news, but she knew there had been something going on, something violent and radical earlier in the winter, although how far from the little fishing village of Dos Palmas and the Paloma Blanca she did not know. President Clinton, free trade—she neither knew nor cared about the details, and Melanie hadn't mentioned it at all when she pressed Camelia into service that night at Casa Abuelita. Nor had Luis or Chris or anyone else since she'd been in Dos Palmas. She had long since forgotten about it.

But now, as they continued further into the jungle, she began to feel edgy and alert. She waited for even the slightest mention of gunfire or curfews by the woman who said she had been there. Perhaps, seeking a Spanish teacher, she had ignored the bodies of protestors freshly executed and randomly littering a picturesque zocalo, their blood staining dusty streets once colored only by hibiscus and bougainvillea. The woman moved quickly onto another topic; Camelia sipped some lukewarm water against the sudden closing of her throat and tried to relax. The grotesque and unexpected vision receded, but she knew it was still there, ghost-like.

"So here's a little more of what you can expect," Chris said loudly in his practiced tour-guide voice, his eyes on the road. "The villagers usually spend several days drinking their homemade mezcal or pulque before the men put on costumes and masks and dance day and night in a series of traditional rituals, stopping only when they finally pass out. By the time we head back to the coast tonight, there will probably be bodies in an exhausted, drunken stupor lining the streets in every village we drive through." In her mind's eye, Camelia could see them, minus only the red flowering of blood on their white shirts to separate them from their fallen brothers in Chiapas. Her ears began to ring. A film of sweat rose on her forehead, dripped into her eyes.

"We're going to stop in a little while," Chris continued, raising his voice over the rattling of the van against the rocky surface. "I have some Mixtec Indian friends waiting for us. They don't see many white people up here; it's a little off the beaten path, tourism-wise."

Camelia knew her *¡Muy bonito!* and *¿Donde está el baño?* were good enough to get by with at the beach, but Chris warned them that up here, where the old ways persisted, few people spoke as much Spanish even as tourists did. Fewer still had a *baño* in their house. Her head buzzed; they had long since left the open horizon of the beach behind them, along with its cooling breeze. The higher up they went, the more the heat and humidity made her groggy and slow.

Maybe it was better after all for her to be crawling up these mountains to the middle of nowhere than being anywhere near the beach. Or, especially, Mel's Shake Shack. She wasn't exactly sure how yesterday afternoon had taken such a bad turn, but she did remember wiping her tear-swollen eyes in front of a clouded mirror in the bar's bathroom, Eric's voice ringing in her ears. He had disappeared like smoke; she struggled with the balky lock on her casita door alone, drunk and heavyhearted.

Eric: suntanned, sinewy arms resting on the gritty saloon table, his eyes the color of the sea though ringed slightly in red and bookended with crow's feet. What a story, as though he could make all the bad things go away by simply pretending they didn't exist. And yet he had steadied her for a moment. He seemed earthbound, a serious child who would hold tightly to the string on a helium balloon while still enjoying it as it floated in the wind. She felt lightheaded, not unlike a balloon herself, and absently brushed at a patch of road dust the color of new pennies on her legs. Soft and fine, the dry powder stuck to her skin, her clothes, her lips. With every sip from her water bottle, she tasted the road in the back of her throat. She willed herself away from yesterday, instead to be drawn into today and the rocky moonscape they drove through, baking under a painfully blue sky.

"It hardly seems much different from New Mexico." She hadn't intended to say it out loud, and the sound of her voice surprised her. Chris laughed.

"Of course it would be similar; it was once all the same country, wasn't it? Arbitrary political borders don't change the geography."

Most of the rugged countryside they passed through seemed uninhabited, save for evidence of some rudimentary farming activity and the occasional fence post made from a crooked tree, strung with sagging barbed wire perhaps a generation ago. A *campesino* dressed in immaculate white, his dark skin etched in sun-baked rivulets not unlike the road itself, appeared with a heavily laden burro. Where he came from and where he was going—barefoot on the sharp, stony road—were a mystery to her. If there was even a shack made of palm fronds and corrugated tin nearby, it was too well hidden for her to see.

The deeper they got into the mountain wilderness, the more grateful Camelia was for the sturdy old van, which Chris assured them was not unlike a cheap Timex ("Takes a licking and keeps on ticking," he said with a laugh). Expertly navigating the ruts and occasional deep fissures that made up the road, he treated the van as their tank, their protection. It was also a target: Chris seemed to expect it when they were stopped at an impromptu roadblock made of large stones rolled strategically across the road. A ragged group of children, some of them still maneuvering the last rock into the roadway, begged him for a donation for medical expenses for a little friend who had been hit by just such a van while playing too close to the road the day before, or so he said.

"These kids were here the last time I came through here," he said, shaking his head when his passengers automatically began reaching for their wallets. He conversed for a moment with a tall, thin boy in a torn Nike T-shirt, who then ordered the smaller children to move the rocks out of the road. They waved and grinned as the van passed.

Like the children's roadblock, the next stop also was not part of their itinerary. A truck waited by the side of the road flanked by two men, perhaps a father and son. Chris slowed the van and had a leisurely chat with them through the open passenger window, then pulled up in front of their truck and parked. He hopped out and continued talking as though they were all good friends. Camelia felt captive without the necessary vocabulary even to be polite, and she gazed out the window away from the scene until her fellow passengers began chattering again. The younger man put one end of a short plastic hose into the van's gas tank and the other in his mouth; a moment later he transferred the hose to a plastic jug.

"Oh, they do this all the time; he knows what he's doing," Chris said with casual reassurance into the window and continued his conversation. Once enough gas filled their jug, they both thanked all of the van's riders profusely and waved for several minutes as Chris headed back up the road.

Finally, they made a sharp turn and entered a tiny village. Chris stopped the VW in the middle of the street and hurried out, imploring the group to stay put while he made a quick inquiry inside. He disappeared into a tiny building hung with the same simple white cotton dresses adorned with embroidery Camelia had seen everywhere since she first landed in Oaxaca. Adobe houses not unlike those she had seen north of Santa Fe lined the few roads. Each structure was made of the same sun-dried earth, looking as though it would one day melt back into the ground, leaving little to speak of its former existence. She could as easily have been somewhere in northern New Mexico as down here at the bottom of the continent.

But at home, she often felt a sense of foreboding. Rampant poverty was evident; heroin had decimated multiple generations of families, and vacant buildings were everywhere, their windows broken, their walls tagged with graffiti. Trash blew across the northern New Mexico llanos like tumbleweeds. Here, laughter escaped from behind woven curtains hanging from every door and window.

Flowers spilled from crudely fashioned window boxes. Smiling women in their intricate *huipils* looked like vibrant tropical birds. Even the many crosses in front of the tiny, windowless chapel were bedecked with flowering vines and bright paint.

". . . and they don't even know they're poor; they live simply and they are very happy." The woman in the seat in front of her had jumped out as soon as Chris told everyone to stay in the van; now she returned with him, a clump of bright fabric rolled under her arm.

"Don't believe that for a second, Mavis. I hope none of you believe that. For every year the families manage to keep a young girl in school, there is one less baby born to strain their meager resources." Chris started the van again, and they threaded their way through the village. Judging by the number of young girls toting babies in their arms or wrapped in rebozos slung around their shoulders, it didn't look to Camelia like the plan was working.

"Let's not be patronizing just because to you they're exotic," Chris added, a tight grin barely softening the edge in his voice.

Tsch-tsch-tsch-tsch . . . Camelia heard the sound long before she could see the dried gourd rattles it came from. Chris hurriedly pulled off the road again and herded his party toward the village zocalo. *Tsch-tsch-tsch-tsch* . . . the dancing had begun. The men were dressed as the invading Spaniards of half a millennium ago, updated with the secondhand business suit and tie of the corporate white man—another loathed invader, Camelia was sure. Topped off with carved, painted masks like ones she had seen in Luis's house and hats of rooster feathers, they stepped in loosely formed routines all along the narrow side streets, slowly making their way to the center of the village.

Step, step, bow, turn, step, step, bow, turn, always accompanied by the *tsch-tsch-tsch* of the rattles. A trio of diablos covered in bright red paint and wearing devil masks ran past Camelia, their bare feet nimbly dancing along the steep, rocky street. Through the rubber soles of her sandals, the ground felt like hot coals.

Tsch-tsch-tsch-tsch . . . the monotonous, rhythmic beat of the rattles held in the hand of every dancer for hours on end remained an unceasing soundtrack for the rest of the long afternoon. In every village they stopped in, on every street, as bottles without labels were passed among dancers and spectators alike, although the steps grew weary, the rattling continued, keeping time, never stopping. Camelia was sure she could still hear it even when they were miles away.

Once, a cluster of barefoot little girls with dirty faces and fingers observed them from a short distance. In frilly dresses, with long hair and tiny earrings, they giggled and pointed. Their focus was not on the dancers but on Camelia and the other light-skinned foreigners. Self-conscious now, her headache thrumming and her throat dry, she wandered to a shady spot across the street, separating herself from her van mates, their cameras, their chattiness.

A few minutes later, Chris disappeared into a house on a nearby corner. Camelia decided to follow, lingering just outside the doorway. She could see an old sewing machine inside the dim room, *huipils* and other garments hanging from nails in the walls, a bolt of fabric leaning against a chair. A woman took the blouse Chris showed her and appeared to measure it, stretching her arm from elbow to wrist along its edge and then laying two fingers at the end.

"*Grande*," he said, his arms spread apart like he was showing the size of a fish he caught; she replied in a language unfamiliar to Camelia. There was a lot of nodding and gesticulating until finally the woman produced a scrap of paper and a nub of pencil and they both went further in to the house. Moments later, Chris returned to the doorway and motioned her inside.

"Come, come; we'll have lunch. Where is everyone?"

She looked back at the street, her eyes not yet adjusted to the brightness after peering into the dark room. Suddenly they were all crowding into the doorway as though they had been there all along. Camelia followed a few steps behind as they trooped through the two-room house, past a table piled with cut fabric, large bobbins of thick thread, a basket of buttons, and out to the tiny, cluttered backyard. A skinny dog chewed on a stale tortilla, oblivious to the activity. Several women bustled about, rinsing dishes in huge urns of murky water before filling them with the contents of several steaming pots. Camelia's stomach lurched. She avoided everyone's eyes and headed back into the house, past the seamstress and Chris, who continued to try to explain his order and barely registered her passage.

"I'll just wait for you guys out here," she murmured as she went out the front door. Two dogs lay prone on the hot street under the meager shade of a jacaranda tree. The dancers moved on, the *tsch-tsch-tsch* hanging in the still air. Her eyes ached behind her sunglasses.

Sitting on a low adobe wall surrounding a dry fountain in yet another village zocalo, Camelia had long ago lost track of how many times they'd stopped, in how many villages they had seen the dancers, heard the rattles. This zocalo— just a small central square serving a village only a few blocks long—was overrun with children chasing one another with colored eggs in their hands. At some invisible signal between themselves, they launched the eggs, showering their target in a jumble of bright confetti and fine ash. Everywhere they ran about, clutching little plastic bags full of the fragile dyed eggshells and their nuisance payload.

She had begun to feel invisible when two little girls approached her; one of them motioned to her to take off her hat and promptly smashed a confetti-filled egg on her head before they both ran off laughing. As if a spell had suddenly broken, Camelia felt herself finally relax. She fingered the confetti in her hair and smiled at the shrieking children.

"We have one more stop to make," Chris told the road-weary group a little while later as they assembled once again at the van. "I need to see a friend in the next village. We've been hearing stories that he's wasting away in an alcoholic stupor while his children are living on nothing but tortillas and salt." He put the van in gear and pulled out onto the main road, away from the dusty zocalo. Camelia began to regret skipping lunch.

After a short ride, they once again trudged out of the van. Mavis and her husband, Eddie, went off in one direction, Chris in another, leaving Camelia with a mostly silent older woman with a nimbus of white hair who had introduced herself as "Sally from New Hampshire" in the van earlier in the day. They stood together on a small platform facing a clearing where several groups of dancers moved in a trancelike state. They were quickly surrounded by young children bored by the dancers.

A little girl of six or seven, incongruous in a red T-shirt instead of the dresses the rest of the girls wore, approached her and, with a touch as soft as moth dust, tapped her arm. Camelia smiled back at her, and the girl leaped away like a long-legged rabbit. A moment later she returned and planted herself next to Camelia, a wide grin on her young face. A maternal ache washed through Camelia, and she reached down to hold the little girl's hand.

Tsch-tsch-tsch-tsch . . . each group of dancers followed its own movements in its respective corner. In front of Sally and Camelia were more of the rooster-tail-capped dancers in business suits. Farther down, a masked group danced in leather chaps and spun lariats. Several adolescent boys dancing in one corner of the yard were dressed as women. Chris had appeared at her side for a moment; he whispered to Camelia that many of the boys in dresses were not just playacting for the holiday, and were well integrated into their community. He headed off again, striding directly across the field and through the clusters of dancers, thoroughly ignored. The little girl standing with her ran after Chris, grabbed his hand, and tugged him toward a small house. Camelia envisioned Chris's friend snoring loudly in a dark room, empty bottles on the floor under his cot, his too-thin children playing in the dirt.

Stepping down from the platform to make their way to another part of the clearing, she and Sally suddenly found themselves in a crowd of *vaqueros*—cowboys—and children who moved shyly out of their way. Before they took more than a few steps, three men confronted them. One, in a T-shirt and leather chaps over his jeans, had oranges stuffed under his shirt for breasts and a mask of a pig face. A second, in a plaid shirt, jeans, and cowboy hat, wore a mask of a wolf, or maybe a demon. The third man, reluctantly pulled along by his friends, was a simple *campesino*, familiar in now-dusty white with a wide straw hat.

The three spoke loudly in a confusing rush of unfamiliar words. Sally stayed mute; Camelia felt hot as the crowd turned toward them, and she tried to back up. The wolf grabbed her arm. "*¿De donde, de donde?*"

She finally understood and, trying to stay calm, she smiled and said, "Oh! *Los Estados Unidos*, of course." She heard her words repeated as they gabbled among themselves, the wolf still holding onto Camelia's arm and pressing in against her and Sally. The two masked men pull their *campesino* friend forward.

"*¡Beso, beso!*" It took her a moment to comprehend: "kiss."

Sally, shaken, was coming visibly undone. "*Muchas gracias, muchas gracias, me gusto*," she started, stepping backward and bowing and nodding to everyone in front of her. Camelia's laugh was nervous. The wolf who had her arm suddenly thrust the *campesino* at her; she could see how drunk he was, they all were. Bottles passed from one to the other. *Tsch-tsch-tsch-tsch* sounded loudly in her ears. Children were laughing; the surging crowd sounded like circling birds. The gentle farmer took her hand, moved to raise it to his lips, and then stumbled. Stupid as fraternity brothers, the three men fell against one another in a rousing chorus of sodden hilarity.

Sally's lip trembled. "*Mucho gusto, por favor, mucho gusto*." Camelia had a sensation of floating. *Tsch-tsch-tsch-tsch*. She could be spirited away in the crowd, laid out on a side street with a red flower blooming between her legs. She could be given the sharp, harsh drink and feel the sting of rusty iron bedposts cutting her palms. She could be carried to the top of a mountain of handmade bricks, offered in appeasement for a blessing of rain. She could rise above the crowd and drift away like smoke.

A tiny hand slid into Camelia's and pulled; with heavy eyes she saw the little girl in the red T-shirt. Yanking her other arm away from the men, who were busily kissing her hand and guffawing, Camelia grabbed Sally, and the three of them snaked away in the crowd to the van, where Chris was waiting with Mavis and Eddie. Chris threaded the van carefully through the streets as eggs—raw eggs, and then some rocks—flew at them.

The girl in the red T-shirt ran alongside the van, her smile fresh and innocent as sunrise, and disappeared.

Sally cried silently and rocked herself to sleep. Camelia fingered the handful of pesos in her pocket and thought of the girl eating tortillas and salt for dinner.

10 Mi Casa Es Su Casa

Eric rubbed his fingers around the edge of his plate, littered with the remains of a crumbly fish taco. The restaurant of the Hotel Paloma Blanca was mellow; among its handful of tables, only a few patrons lingered over after-dinner drinks, their laughter subdued. Candles flickered on the neatly set tabletops, and handwoven napkins stirred slightly in the breeze. Laced with a sweet breath of night air coming off the ocean, everything—chairs, tables, even the flatware—had a slight coating of moisture.

He thought of the thin, dry air of New Mexico, so devoid of even marginal amounts of humidity. Sometimes it seemed as though one's very soul could dry up and blow away.

And yet, one could experience a certain clarity of vision in New Mexico, where everything soft and loose and smooth was stripped away and reality was as hard and quick as a rattlesnake bite. It was a clarity he was beginning to miss, and the thought of living in Santa Fe again flashed across his mind like the fragment of a barely remembered dream.

Well, it wasn't as though he was going to do anything about it tonight. He reached across the table for his cigarettes and was just putting them in his pocket when movement near the door caught his eye. A languid Camelia had appeared, with the hint of a smile when she saw him. He motioned her over, pushing his plate aside, and put the cigarettes back on the table.

Her hair curled gently around her face; her eyes were dark as the night around them. She wore a red dress with large white flowers splashed across it, some kind of silky material that draped over her lean body with the fluid grace of water. She almost floated, devoid of the tension that had seemed to hold her very limbs together the day before. He signaled to Patricio to get her a drink as she approached.

"Have a seat, *señorita*. You look like you need it. Been out with Chris and his little caravan today?"

Esperanza had told him this morning about Chris's planned excursion into the mountains with his old van full of tourists, Camelia included. For a brief moment he had considered closing the café and joining them, but the vision of her tear-stained face in the bar yesterday afternoon still hung in his mind, and he had gone back to squeezing oranges before the morning's rush.

"Yeah. It was something." She settled in the chair across from him and stretched her legs out under the table. Patricio delivered her drink and took his time strolling back to the bar; he planted himself facing them, his arms crossed.

"On the way back, we were stopped by a bunch of guys in some kind of mismatched uniforms. They had automatic weapons." Her voice quavered, and her fingers shook as she squeezed a *limone* into her glass and sipped her mezcal. "They poked around in the van for a few minutes, but Chris talked to them, and they let us pass. He never said who they were. I took a long shower after we got back."

"Yeah, that happens sometimes around here. More so lately, I suppose." He offered her a cigarette, lit it for her, watched her lips as she inhaled. She was not a habitual smoker, he could tell.

"Looks like you're already done here. Sorry; I hope I'm not disturbing you."

"Not at all," he said, choosing not to add anything at all about just how much she had already disturbed him. "Patricio, *una Coke para mí, por favor?*"

"Coke?" Patricio replied from across the small room, his eyebrows lifting. He had done the same thing an hour earlier, when Eric ordered his dinner without his customary mezcal shots on the side.

"*Sí, amigo*: Coca-Cola. You've heard of it?"

Eric shot him a pointed look, but Patricio's surprise was justified. He had drunk enough mezcal in the last three years to send his liver floating for a lifetime on an agave sea. Mezcal was not his own private vice; his drinking, like everything else, was everybody's business in Dos Palmas. And yet he knew he'd had his last drink—of anything— yesterday while sitting with Camelia in the Punto de Luz. He had looked at the sticky glass in his hand while she cried in the *baño*, and while there was no connection whatsoever that he could see, even so, he had said, "No more." In that moment, he knew he meant it.

It was not the first time. Years ago, dragging himself out of New York, he had determined to go as far away as he could from one more needle, one more night in a stinking, crumbling squat. That time, before he let himself sell it for one more fix, he instead rode his bike heading west until he ran out of gas. He slept in a field for two days, waking only to vomit. He walked the bike for miles until he found a gas station; he ran cold water over his head in the bathroom sink; he drank a gallon of Gatorade. He survived.

Last night was nothing. He swayed all night in the hammock, awake and anxious. This morning his hands shook so hard he couldn't hold the knife to cut the oranges for juice. But already he was feeling clearer. Calmer. So this is what the ocean looks like in the moonlight. So this is what the night air smells like.

And this is what a beautiful woman looks like. Desire suddenly caught flame inside him. So many different emotions and expressions danced across her face, easier around the edges now that she'd relaxed, that Eric could hardly take his eyes off her. Patricio had brought her more mezcal along with his Coke; she reached for the full shot glass from Patricio, but he didn't release it at first.

"Go slow, *señorita*," he reminded her. "*Es una buena medicina*; there's no rush." She nodded, blushing, and watched Patricio squeeze the *limón* into her glass and set it on the table in front of her before strolling away. She smiled gently at Eric. Oh, he was falling, he knew it now. *Falling, falling, falling . . .*

". . . hey, you want security, go to jail—that's the way I look at it," Camelia was saying, her tongue slipping over the words with mock toughness, her hand just missing knocking the glass off the table. "I can't see a life without risk. I don't mean you have to jump out of an airplane. That's just stupid. The most dangerous thing in the world? Relationships. Just trying to be honest about your feelings to yourself and to someone else is absolutely terrifying, but what else are you going to do? Pretend you don't feel anything? Pretend you *do*?"

Ah. Here she was sitting across the table from him, trying to justify running headlong into exactly the kind of thing he always found himself running fast away from. She would have no argument from him tonight about how terrifying that was. Her eyes were loose, her cheeks, flushed. She crushed the cigarette out and leaned in toward Eric; underneath the mezcal and lime, he was intensely aware of the scent of her skin and the salt air, sweet and heavy with the scent of night-blooming tropical flowers.

"I want nothing more than to spend the rest of my life lying on that beach out there," she said, her voice barely above a whisper. "I want to sleep with the strong, brown arms of a man around me, and I want to drink the juice of fresh oranges every morning. I want to feel the sun, not just on my back and on my face, but through me, inside of me. I want . . ." Her eyes began to brim; her lips closed. Her plane left tomorrow morning, and he knew she would be on it.

She kissed him on the cheek and walked out of the empty restaurant, steadying herself on the backs of chairs. Something inside him seized up without warning, and he watched her head back to her room with what he recognized, surprised and saddened, as longing, a feeling he thought he had drowned years before. She did not turn or wave. His eyes were burning.

"Hey, old man, buy you a drink?" Chris appeared before him, startling him. He didn't realize he was standing; was he thinking he might actually follow Camelia? To do what, tap on her door while hoping she might have already fallen into a mezcal dream and he could go back to his little cottage on the beach scot-free, shrugging his shoulders with relief? Or to hammer loudly until the other guests poked their heads out their doors at the ruckus, wondering whether getting involved with that loco Brit who makes the smoothies was a good idea or not? He nodded to Chris and sat down, spent.

A smiling Patricio returned yet again to the table, this time with two shots of tequila, before Eric could protest. He watched Chris sip at his drink, looking past him with the absurd hope that Camelia might change her mind and come back.

"So how's business, *amigo*?"

"Good, good. Selling lots of juice, lots of breads, lots of smoothies. Yours?" Eric lit a cigarette. Talk about business was not going to be enough to take his mind off Camelia. There was only one distraction he knew he could rely on, and he toyed with the shot glass in front of him for some time, wondering how long he could hold it before he raised it to his lips.

"Things seem a little quieter than I expected. I suppose it's all that noise in Chiapas keeping tourists away." Chris sighed.

"I haven't noticed anything, but then again, I really don't need much to keep my place open," Eric said. He had good reason for keeping his life and his business so small; it was almost more than he could manage as it was. And while a little revolution nearby wouldn't stop the surfers and young wanderers who made Mel's a daily stop from coming to Dos Palmas, he knew Chris had to count on consistent numbers if he wanted to keep employing the entire village.

"How's Nico these days?" He might as well find out what the hell Chris was up to, anyway. The only time they had spoken of the rest of the family's move to the States last year, Chris had said he wanted to get his kids back to a civilized place before they grew up to be monsters. He had made no mention of Melanie then or since.

Eric wondered suddenly where exactly Camelia fit into the larger Sullivan family picture. Although he was sure she had told him yesterday, he had no idea why she was here now. He lit another cigarette and looked at Chris through the smoke, confusion churning inside him.

"Fine, fine, everybody's fine," Chris replied, helping himself to Eric's untouched drink, his eyes lowered. "I'm putting him on a plane tomorrow with Camelia. He obviously can't stay here, even though he's driving his mother crazy up there. Trying to decide if I should go too. What with this construction debacle going on, it's not really a good time for me to take a break, although I sure could use one."

Eric watched the edges of his cigarette burn and felt a laser-like clarity of purpose begin to form. The two men sat for several moments listening to the waves hit the beach, cocooned in their own thoughts. Finally Chris stood and stretched, shook Eric's hand, and headed out. A few moments later, Eric pushed his chair out from the table, startling the one-eyed cat that had fallen asleep at his feet, and went to find Camelia.

Tall lamps buried in the swaying fronds of the palm trees threw a dim yellowy light on the walkway from the restaurant to the pool. He saw the glow of a citronella candle before he made out her silhouette stretched out on a lounge chair, the lit pool water throwing wavy shadows everywhere. He strolled over to where she sat.

"Trouble sleeping?" He seated himself on a chair next to her, his back to the pool. As his eyes adjusted to the dark, he saw the small bottle in her hand; he could smell the dusky mezcal.

"Nightmares used to really bother me," he said after a moment, thinking again about the life he had left behind in Santa Fe, a life that belonged to someone else.

"Not me." Her voice was quiet, raw. "There are no dreams. It's like the sleep of the dead here. Ten, twelve hours like a stone; I struggle to resurface without having moved all night. At home, I sleep very lightly. I toss and turn, I have snatches of dreams, I wake up at the slightest noise or tiniest bit of light. At my friend Luis's house, in Oaxaca, I couldn't believe it when he told me how the mosquitoes kept him awake and how he listened to the coyotes howling for hours before dawn. I didn't hear a thing."

How necessary the numbing darkness of his alcohol-laced nights had become to his survival in Mexico. Without it, he knew he would sleep very little, but he wouldn't miss those long, dark hours of nothingness. If he couldn't sleep, he would get up and sit in the hammock, listen to the waves, and wait for the early morning birds to salute the first rays of sun. He was ready.

"What will you do when you get back to Santa Fe?" he asked her, gently prying the bottle out of her fingers and placing it underneath his chair. It took her a while to answer, but her words, when they came, were jagged and alert.

"Start over, what else? Move Michael the rest of the way out of my house and out of my life. Find a new job; wait tables, maybe, like everyone else who doesn't know what else to do with themselves. Maybe even leave Santa Fe, I don't know. I thought after I got here that I would formulate some kind of strategy, but that's never really been my strong suit. To be honest, I haven't come up with even one realistic course of action beyond trying for a fresh start. I'm just going to go back and live my life. Get my shit together. Grow up. One thing I do know: life's too long to spend it doing what you don't want to do."

Eric listened to the waves in the distance. He heard a lone taxicab pull into the alley alongside the hotel and discharge its drunken quarry. He noted the breeze in the palm fronds, felt the petals of a vine's flower as it fell from the wall onto his lap, smelled the chlorine from the pool. He placed one hand on her ankle and lightly stroked her bare leg for several moments until she stirred, reaching for him. He leaned forward and buried his face in the hollow of her throat, his hands caught in her hair, his lips sinking gently into the softness of her neck. A moan, buried so deep he could feel it rising inside of him moments before he heard it, escaped him. She held him fast.

The moon had already begun to set, although it was still hours before dawn. Eric hurried along the quiet village roads, a small flashlight casting its beam at his feet. He was pretty sure he knew where he was going. He had been to Esperanza's home several times, but never in the dark, never on foot, never sober. He saw no one. Occasionally a dog barked as his illuminated footfalls transmitted his ghostly presence. The palms rustled. Somewhere a coconut fell to the ground.

When he had left Camelia's room, pulling the door closed gently so as not to wake her, he was a drowning man who had been pulled ashore. He wanted to fall to his knees on the dark beach, fill his fingers with the cold sand. Her hands had clutched him with the fervor of a rescue mission, yet in the moments after he left her, he wasn't sure which of them had been saved and which had done the saving.

Now, with the determination of the newly reborn, he planted one foot in front of the other along the dark road. Eric knew Esperanza would be up. Her house would be the one enveloped with the aroma of freshly baked breads. A fire would be lit in the oven outside; perhaps there would be a lantern over the handmade wooden table where she sank her hands into the dough, kneading and turning and patting it with the patience of a short, brown Buddha. In his mind's eye he pictured Miguel in the yard in front of the house, reaching into the adobe oven with a long-armed paddle, removing a tray of fresh loaves in the small, personal sizes Eric had shown them he wanted for Mel's and bringing them inside the house.

Eric strained in the dark to see details among the many mud and tin huts set in the grove of palms until he finally decided to close his eyes and follow his nose. Soon enough, the sweet scent of baking bread told him to turn at the next roughly cut corner, and there he found Esperanza and Miguel just as he had imagined, their faces illuminated in the red heat of the outdoor oven as Miguel pulled out a tray of *pan dulce*. Eric pocketed his flashlight and stood in the dark road in front of the humble two-room casita for a moment. Three small children slept on a thin mattress on the tiny front portal, and two more swayed gently in a hammock. Before he could change his mind, he strode into the arc of firelight from the oven door.

"*¿Señor, qué pasó?*" Esperanza looked stricken. He saw their careworn faces, their hands still busy carving out a living in the middle of the night no matter how inconvenient it might be. Miguel said nothing, but gestured to the front door. Eric knew Miguel could not allow his *patrón* to visit, even at 2:00 a.m., without offering him a drink or some food. Eric declined with a soft "*Muchas gracias, mi amigo,*" then reached into his pocket. He was grateful to have made the journey without running into any stray bandidos, who would have hit the jackpot with him.

"*Aquí esta la llave del café.*" He noted with small pleasure that his outstretched hand was steady. "*Y aquí esta la llave de mi casa en la playa.*" The café and house keys sparkled in the firelight.

Suddenly, absurdly, Eric remembered a moment back in New Mexico, when he had opened a gift given to him and Shelley when Zane was born. It was a potholder—silly, really—in the shape of a tortilla. On its front were inscribed the words *Mi Casa Es Su Casa*. The rusty taste of Chimayó red chile hung in the back of his throat.

"*Y aquí hay dinero extra, en caso que quieres cerrar el café. Gracias por todo.*" He realized he didn't care what they did with this largesse: they could keep the café and make a decent living, or close it and live simply for years on the thick wad of pesos he handed Miguel. It mattered little to Eric, who felt as light as a child's soap bubble floating in the breeze.

Esperanza let him hug her. She held her hands, covered with flour and dough, stiffly out at her sides. He shook Miguel's hand hard and then hugged him too. Esperanza came to life, pressing a hot loaf of bread in his hands, and whispered "*Vaya con Dios*" in his ear before rushing inside in tears. In a moment he was retracing his steps, heading back to his little house on the beach, already no longer his. He had never bothered to lock it; he was surprised he had been able to find the key.

His only plan: to throw a few essentials and his long-unused woodworking tools into the back of his truck and head north, leaving the rest to Esperanza and Miguel, or, no matter, to the sand and the wind and the summer rains. His feet skipped surely across the crude road.

11 The Hardest Blow

Chris sat in a weathered wooden chair on the small portal in front of his casita and listened to the waves in the dark. A note in each room urged the guests to turn their inside and outside lights off as early as possible in the evening to discourage mosquitoes; it seemed that for once they had all complied. The chair was more comfortable than he remembered. In fact, he didn't know when he last had the chance to sit out here in the dark, a couple of shots of tequila zinging through his blood and his feet up on the railing.

Helluva thing about Eric, he thought idly as he listened to the murmurs of a couple of guests heading down the path toward the bar. A man who seemed thoroughly at peace with his simple, almost regimented lifestyle and yet was still grievously tortured. Chris had noted with a surprise he was careful not to show that Eric didn't drink the tequila Chris ordered for him earlier that evening.

He seemed strangely alert, with a sharp edge Chris was unaccustomed to. He also found Eric to be somewhat preoccupied, and it took him some moments to make the connection between the slightly swaying Camelia he had just said good-night to on his way into the restaurant and Eric's presence at a table with empty glasses and a full ashtray.

Trouble. Oh, trouble trouble trouble, Chris thought now as he pictured the possibility of an untethered Camelia and Eric the solitary beach bum together. The whole idea of marriage made women crazy and men flee; why hadn't we figured out, as a species, how to eliminate it entirely by now? He listened to the palm fronds rustle in the wind. If her husband had left for good, as Luis had said on the phone, then it was probably for the best. As things like this go, at least her reality check was swift; no kids, no shared property, everybody could move on quickly. But Eric?

Ah, who am I to talk about trouble anyway, Chris acknowledged. Maybe they're perfect for each other. He had his own troubles. Nico had not reappeared; in fact, although his presence was acute, he had been conspicuously absent since their first, unpleasant meeting last week on the beach. There Chris had been, wrapped in a blanket with Cissy—it was Cissy, wasn't it? Cissy? Missy? Sherrie?—supposedly watching the sunrise although obviously still half-asleep and none too sober yet, when who should quite literally stumble across them in the dawn light but his own goddamned son, assumed to be a thousand miles away in snowy Santa Fe with his mother? They didn't even exchange words. Was it too much to hope for, the idea that perhaps Nico didn't recognize him in the morning darkness?

Chris knew Nico had been in the casita on and off throughout the week, though. His backpack lay where it had been flung in a corner. A dirty T-shirt, a damp towel, a pair of flip-flops all reminded Chris that he was not alone here; whatever little bubble of privacy he thought he might have cultivated had been irrevocably pierced.

Tomorrow would come soon enough. Getting Nico on that plane with Camelia and back to Santa Fe was now an imperative. How he was going to do it, he had no idea. First things first, though. Abruptly he pushed himself out of the chair and went inside. He flipped on the light switch—the hell with the mosquitoes—and grabbed Nico's backpack from the floor, dumping its contents on the bed. Jesus, the kid didn't even bring clean underwear. He rifled through the assortment of cassette tapes and battered Walkman, candy bar wrappers, a dog-eared *Rolling Stone*, a wadded-up T-shirt, until he found what he was looking for: Nico's wallet, a cheap billfold worn around the edges and holding little more than his driver's license and a few bucks. And the credit card Chris was sure he would find.

There it was, Chris Nico Sullivan emblazoned on the Visa card. Fuck that kid anyway; he dropped the wallet back on the bed. He wondered where the bills were going. For all he knew, they were coming right here to the hotel and Emiliana in the front office had been paying them all along.

"As soon as Nico graduates, I'm out of here; I promise I'll come back to the beach and stay." He could hear Melanie whispering in his ear, as she had so many times before in Santa Fe. They had sat on cushions on the floor in front of the fireplace, sipping hot spiced cider spiked with dark rum. "Can't we get him in some kind of accelerated program so he'd finish sooner?" he'd ask. It was their little joke. Nico was more likely to get thrown out than to graduate; the idea of an accelerated program for him was absurd, unless it was putting him on the fast track to dropping out. Their plan had been to hold out until—or more likely *if*—Nico graduated next year, and then figure out a way to rebuild their once-peaceful life in Dos Palmas. But Rayne, suddenly a teenager and full of bullshit just like her brother, had pretty effectively monkey wrenched that idea not too long ago, and now he had no clue what the next few years, months, or even days would hold.

"Hey, what the fuck are you doing with my stuff?" Nico stood in the doorway. Chris could clearly see that although his son was annoyed, he was too stoned to do much about it. The boy stood unsteadily against the doorjamb, his red eyes slitted in the bright room.

"You goddamn punk." Chris's hand folded around the credit card as though it were a weapon. He struggled to find the right words, any words, that would hold him to the ground, weigh him down with some kind of thoughtful adult consideration, some semblance of parental foresight or concern—anything but what he felt surging up inside him, propelling him across the room to grab Nico, missing his throat by millimeters, and settling for a fistful of T-shirt instead.

Nico grabbed Chris's wrist and pulled his father's hand off his shirt with teenage strength Chris had underestimated. Chris almost lost his footing and was astonished to find himself tussling with the boy, who charged him with a rage that had sprung full blown. Pressed back against the wall, Chris felt the breath knocked out him; before he could think, his fist connected with the boy's cheekbone. A chair clattered against the floor tiles and Nico stumbled out the door.

Chris, spent, shook his sore hand and tried to catch his breath. He righted the chair and turned off the light. What the fuck. A man pushing forty should never fight with a teenaged boy. The older man will always lose, no matter who lands the hardest blow.

He reached into a cabinet and pulled out a small bottle of the best painkiller he knew. Forgoing even a glass, he tipped the bottle to his lips and drank, feeling the harsh liquor burn through the gathering storm that had been building in him all weekend. He shoved Nico's things back into the backpack, then went back onto the porch taking the bottle with him, holding it tightly lest it slip through his fingers like everything else he touched.

How men ruin the lives of the very people they need most in this world. Why do we do it? He thought of Melanie, his sweet and dearest love since they were in seventh grade together in grim Portland, now sitting alone in a cold house in blustery February Santa Fe, never the same bright Santa Fe he enjoyed returning to in August or October, and, he finally admitted, no longer the same Melanie he had convinced to run away with him to Mexico so long ago. They had vowed to live forever "on a warm beach far away from the rain," yes, they had.

Nico was in fact conceived on this very beach that was right in front of him tonight, long before there was such a thing as the Hotel Paloma Blanca. But Chris's strategy to save his son's adolescent soul last year by returning the entire family to Santa Fe—after discovering the boy's habit of stealing from tourists—had gone to naught because of his own long absences from home. Melanie's heart broke every day, he knew; with all that energy spent in trying to control Nico, Rayne just slipped right through the cracks. Even if Nico were at home now, where he belonged, Chris knew things wouldn't be any better.

The boy's Spanish came in handy at first as he defended himself from the tough Hispanic kids at school in Santa Fe, but Chris never expected it to serve as his entry into a gang of homeboys who, Chris and Melanie were pretty sure, were involved in several instances of petty thievery in their own neighborhood. They prayed he wouldn't get caught, even as they lectured him, punished him, grounded him, tried to cut him off from his delinquent friends.

Chris put his fingers to his eyes. At least they had Rayne, or so they had thought. Rayne—bright beyond her years and quieter than any Sullivan Chris could remember—became frustrated and then obsessive and entranced with a school project on family trees. It was easy for the local kids to present generations of personal history; Santa Fe was like a living museum, populated mostly with the descendants of Spanish conquistadors and the Native Americans they did battle with.

But instead of making new friends and going to parties, quiet Rayne had spent all her time making numerous trips to the library and poring over Irish, Scottish, and English history books. She sent away to far-flung parishes for family documents, wrote to every relative Chris and Melanie could remember, and saved her babysitting money for what was supposed to be an eighth-grade graduation trip to Great Britain. She knew full well her parents were scheming to find a way to return to Dos Palmas full-time. Chris had made the mistake of ignoring his suspicion that she had no intention of going with them.

Without warning, a warmth began spreading through Chris' body that had nothing to do with mezcal. He knew he was directly responsible for the mess his family had become. And he had no idea what to do about it.

He listened to the sound of the waves in the dark. God, how he loved it here, feeling the warm air on his skin, peering through the darkness at the stars and the shadows of the palm trees. He remembered vividly that night he and Melanie had spent on this beach sixteen years ago: they had left their hammock strung between two trees, two palms that he passed by every day now, and gone down to the sand, still warm from the day's sun. A full moon had illuminated the entire beach.

Oh, how things had changed. Chris now spent most of his time in Mexico engaged in legal battles, fighting everyone from tourism officials and resort big shots to a small troop of construction workers imported from up the coast. His need for simplicity was shattered on a daily basis as he was confronted with the constant struggle for hygiene in the restaurant kitchen, the proper accounting of cash in the till.

If he were to lose his current gamble with the Mexican government, what would happen to Dos Palmas? He had a bold plan to quietly expand his tiny operation—currently just the few casitas and the restaurant—by adding a larger building with several deluxe rooms further up the hillside and then doubling the meager size of the eatery. He had heard rumors of a planned publicity blitz by the government's tourism department to attract a more upscale tourist to the area around Dos Palmas, instead of the ragtag hippie surfers and wanderers who had made this last shred of pristine Mexican coastline their own. He wanted to be ready.

But when his first pad of concrete was finally poured, after he was sure he had paid off everyone necessary to get the job done, the suits from Mexico City descended on the coast and threatened to shut down the whole business. One afternoon he was sitting in his own cozy restaurant enjoying some guacamole with a honey-brown college girl on an extended winter break, and the next thing he knew a dozen Resort del Mundo honchos were strolling loudly through his property, guided by those same tourism officials from Mexico City who had smilingly pocketed handfuls of his cash.

He knew what was coming next. The telephones and faxes, espresso machines and deliveries of purified ice had already become necessary, desirable. He couldn't run his business without them anymore. And it would be nice when his driveway and the other peripheral roads were paved and lined with streetlights (even if they wouldn't work) and wire trash cans (that no one would use). But what then?

Whether he was able to hold onto his tiny corner of paradise or not, yes, he knew what was coming; he watched it happening. Already many villagers had abandoned their subsistence fishing and farming and moved onto the beach to sell pilfered Cokes and refilled bottles of fetid tap water to tourists, the sort who were used to more creature comforts than the usual batch of lost souls and sun worshippers, escapees from the very kind of tourism that was sure to follow.

I wanted to get away from it all, he thought, the bottle growing slick in his sweating hand, but it seems I've brought it all along with me. Isn't that always the way. A bottled-water truck rumbled down the alley next to the hotel property, and Chris looked into the darkness with defeated eyes. It's no different than what I left behind, no different at all.

He took another long swallow of mezcal. He remembered a conversation he and Eric had had over drinks one night not long ago as they commiserated over the changing tides of their little village on the beach.

"It's just the same as anyplace else," Eric had said, his voice as nonchalant as the wave he directed to the bartender for another shot. "The opportunity to make a buck brings out the best in some people and the worst in others. Aspen. Key West. Provincetown. Santa Fe. Progress, if you want to call it that, would have come to

Dos Palmas whether you built that hotel or not. You did a good thing here, you had the right idea when you started. It's not your fault it got out of control. It's just like anyplace else: you try to take care of your own and do the best you can, but you can't be responsible for every moron who shows up to ruin things."

Chris had gone back to his casita later that night with a young surfer, tattoos of roses and moons wreathed around both her wrists, hundreds of tiny beads clicking and clacking in her braided hair. He didn't want to think about Santa Fe or everything he was trying to escape when he and Melanie had come to Dos Palmas in the first place.

Now the fate of the village kept him awake nights and hovered around the periphery of his mind during his workday. It itched like a stubborn scab, one he couldn't resist picking at even though it caused him great distress every time he did. His head began to ache. What the hell was he doing here, anyway? His family needed him now, not in some distant future when he could present them an uncomplicated life after spending endless days working the bugs out of this impossible system he'd created.

Chris struggled out of his chair and made his way back inside the casita, drunker than he had been in a long time. He felt burdened with more baggage than any one man could bear, yet his face burned at the memory of the solace he had so frequently indulged in—the endless supply of unattached women, the quiet trips up the mountain to visit with the tight native families and the artisans, the lost weekends down the coastline in more rustic villages as yet undiscovered by the corporate resort suits but filled with a delicious assortment of carefree, adventurous young people always on the go. And now, this trouble over in San Cristóbal. Was that going to bleed into Oaxaca too, all the way to the beach perhaps? Free trade, right; the whole thing smelled bad to him. Sometimes he wished he could just walk away from the Hotel Paloma Blanca, just walk away into the mountains or into the sea.

"Oh, right, and then what?" he said out loud to the empty room, slamming the spent bottle into the little trash can in the corner, where it tinkled into pieces. A staff of sixteen and their families depended on the Hotel Paloma Blanca for a livelihood that now ranked far beyond their dreams. Sixteen, soon to be fourteen, that is, once he got around to firing brothers Guillermo and Bonifacio, who now spent their late afternoon maintenance shifts out on the beach, selling *cervezas* stolen right off his delivery truck to the surfers.

And then there were his suppliers—the craftspeople who made everything from the bricks to the furniture, from the curtains and bedspreads to the plates used in the restaurant. And the fishermen who brought kilos of fresh seafood to his door daily. And all those itinerant entrepreneurs who had suddenly shown up on the beach, selling sodas and beers, *cacahuates* and tamales, beads and silver rings, even hair-braiding services to the travelers who came to Dos Palmas in greater and greater numbers every year. Thank God the cartels were clustered further north; drug gangs, that would be all they needed here to make the whole place a ghost town overnight.

Eric. Now Eric had the right idea, Chris thought, counting the floor tiles that would take him into the back bedroom as soon as he could walk without falling. Just a simple little café, only one employee depending on him, no family, no responsibilities. If he wanted to close up shop for a day to go play on the beach or drive up into the mountains, he could, although it wasn't as though he ever would.

Chris steadied himself at the table and shuffled into the bedroom, only once needing to reach out to the wall to keep himself upright before he could fall luxuriously into bed. That Eric, driving away from Santa Fe and his whole life without a clue as to what he would do next or where he would go or what his family would do without him, and look at him now, he'd reinvented himself, he'd started over with a clean slate, it can be done, it can be done . . .

12 We Have Plenty of Time

The bedsheets held Eric's scent—cigarette smoke, the particular musk of the ocean, sweet night-blooming jasmine—long after he left Camelia's bed. She stretched, catlike, feeling every limb and muscle anew. The marching band in the hills had begun to play. If only she had coffee, she would never leave the bed again. If only she did not have to go back to Santa Fe.

In a moment not unlike the chaotic one that had propelled her out of her house before dawn a lifetime ago, she remembered she had a flight to catch. Grabbing the pile of rumpled clothing from the chair and jamming it into her bag, she rescued her still-damp bathing suit from the bathroom sink and scooped up last night's dress from the floor without a second glance, shoving them into the bag as well. Pulling on a stray T-shirt and a pair of jeans, she thrust her feet into her sandals and ran out the door, hat and sunglasses both askew.

"*¿Sí, señorita?*" Emiliana sat behind the desk of the front office, her eyes glued to a faded copy of *People* magazine.

"Ah, *sí*, yes, *¿un taxi, por favor? Al aeropuerto?*" Camelia rummaged through her bag for her plane ticket. "I'm kind of in a hurry; I think I might miss my plane."

"Chuey waits in the alley every morning. The plane leaves at eleven—I think you have a few minutes. It's not far." Emiliana's English was barely accented; she languidly turned the page of her magazine.

"Chuey?"

"Chuey, *¿el taxista?*" Without lifting her eyes from the page, she pointed down the brick pathway toward the alley.

"Oh, sí, of course, yes, thank you. And Señor Chris. *¿Está aquí?*"

"He will go with you to the airport with Nico. He might even be in Chuey's taxi right now, waiting for you." She finally looked up at Camelia, her gaze sly.

Unnerved, Camelia stumbled her way through the thick greenery to the alley. What a fishbowl this place was; how could Chris stand it? The same taxi driver who had picked her up at the airport a few days ago leaned on the hood of the green station wagon; Chris and Nico were nowhere in sight.

"Ah, *señorita*, no need to rush; we have plenty of time, at least five minutes." Chuey made no move to take her bag; instead he finished his cigarette and tossed the butt into the alley. Camelia flung her duffle in the open rear window and silently climbed into the back seat. Eric's teeth on her neck, his hands stroking her from shoulder to ankle with the tender sureness of ownership . . . she closed her eyes, resting her head against the window.

"Chuey, *por favor*, hold up, man!" Chris came crashing through the hibiscus dragging a struggling Nico by the arm. The boy had a backpack slung over his shoulder and a bruise on his cheek. Chris looked as though he had fallen into his clothes from five thousand feet.

"*Gracias*, man, sorry about that." Chris grabbed the door handle and shoved Nico in the back seat next to her, shutting the door so quickly, Camelia started. She looked at the miserable boy as he stared out the window, his lip trembling, his cheekbone a mottled green. Her stomach flipped, and she bit the inside of her lip. She wanted to reach over and touch him, put her arms around him, something.

Chris got in the front seat and Chuey gunned the engine; a plume of dust from the road shot up behind them. Camelia felt panic rise in her chest and tried to control her breathing.

"So, Señor Chris, what has happened to your *amigo*, the *gringo loco* at Mel's?" Chuey's voice cut through Camelia like a spear; fine golden hairs rose on her arms.

"*No se.* I saw him last night in the restaurant, and he was sober as a sea turtle. Never seen anything like it." Chris's arm hung over the back of the seat, his fingers twitching. He had yet to acknowledge her, but Camelia was sure he would reach to grab Nico if he had too. She inched herself closer to her door.

"Oh, well, he's your friend, so I thought you knew," Chuey said with a disinterest Camelia knew was feigned. She also suspected his English was for her benefit—she had noticed the locals always spoke Spanish to Chris. She wouldn't be surprised if they both already knew Eric was with her last night.

"Knew what, Chuey?" Chris was irritable and edgy; Nico hadn't moved.

"Why, *señor*, only that he did not open Mel's this morning."

Chris looked at Chucy and then glanced at Camelia in the back seat. She turned to the window.

"What the fuck are you talking about, man?"

They were on the airport tarmac now. Chuey made an elaborate dance out of pulling the station wagon as close as he could to a solitary orange traffic cone without knocking it over, only a few feet from the little plane.

"Chuey?"

Camelia felt Chris's eyes on her as she slowly adjusted her hat and her sunglasses, smoothed down her wrinkled T-shirt, opened the door.

"*Ayii, señor, no se*. Esperanza, she opened up with his keys and never said a word about Señor Eric. It was Miguel who squeezed the oranges. Don't forget your bag, *señorita*." His eyes in the rearview mirror pinned her; his shiny silver grin turned her stomach.

Camelia grabbed her duffle from the back and slammed the car door. Just a few more minutes, and she would be sitting on the plane with Nico, watching as the sapphire coastline receded below them. She would sink into her seat and savor her memories and sort out what to do when she got home. She would drink nothing but Coke or cold water.

Nico stayed in the car until Chris opened the door and pulled him out. The pilot stood outside the plane, watching the propeller as it started up.

"Listen, Camelia, thanks again; tell Melanie—" Chris started, but suddenly Nico twisted out of his grasp.

"Fuck you, I told you I'm not going unless you go!" he yelled, and then in a split second he turned and ran across the tarmac toward a jungle of palm trees.

"Oh my God, Nico!" Camelia felt the day unravel.

"Oh, *Jesucristo*, not again," Chris, deflated, slapped both hands over his eyes; his legs buckled beneath him.

"Shit, are you OK?" She bent toward him, her heart pumping wildly. She couldn't get her bearings: should she run after Nico, stay with Chris, get on the plane, or, why not, just spread out on the hot tarmac like a lizard until the whole sorry, sideways day was over?

"Señor Chris? Do you want me to follow him?" Chuey called out the window of the taxi.

Chris sighed deeply after a moment and slowly pushed himself up. Camelia reached over to help him. "Oh, in a minute, Chuey, I'll go with you. We have plenty of time. He won't get far."

She eyed the puddle jumper; the pilot still stood there, hands in his pockets, watching them. The engine grew louder.

"You might as well go, Camelia. It's the only flight out, and if you miss it you'll be stuck with us for another day," Chris said finally, signaling to the pilot with a wave. "Don't worry about Nico—he's my kid, and I'll take care of it. Just tell Melanie . . . well, tell Melanie, if you don't mind please, that I've got everything under control and I'll get Nico home as soon as I can. I'll get him on the plane tomorrow morning, or I'll drive him to Oaxaca and put him on a plane there, or I'll bring him home myself—whatever—but I'll take care of it." He turned back to the taxi.

"I'll tell Eric you said good-bye." He tossed the words out the window as they pulled away suddenly. "That is, if I can find him." She stood stone still on the tarmac, dust from the car rising around her like fog.

"*¡Señorita, señorita!*" the pilot called to her from the plane, rousing her, and she rushed to the rickety metal steps, one hand holding down her hat, the other dragging her duffle.

PART III

13 Let the Fates Decide

Her old Wagoneer slogged its way up La Bajada, the long, steep hill marking the entry into Santa Fe from the lower elevations of the south. Even at this late hour, there was enough traffic on the highway to make Camelia nervous. Semis that usually dragged along in the slow lane were passing her; she gripped the wheel tightly. Finally, she crested the hill and saw the city lights spread out below. Knowing the foothills of the Sangre de Cristos were dark and stable behind them, she let herself relax. Home.

Dos Palmas to Oaxaca. Oaxaca to Mexico City. Mexico City to Houston. Houston to Albuquerque. She had escaped any clear thought about what lay ahead by dozing on every flight, yet she felt unrested and anxious. Eric, his hands, his body: the memory, this morning so fresh she could still taste his skin on her tongue, had receded like the tide in the netherworld of constant travel. Her whole life had turned upside-down in the space of a week, as though her head had simply checked out and left her body to run things. How did everything come apart so quickly? She drove through the quiet darkness.

Twenty minutes later she was crunching her way over the frozen ruts in her driveway. Several days' worth of carelessly folded newspapers lay scattered on the ground below the mailbox. The house was dark; Michael's truck was not there. She rested her head on the steering wheel. Eric, his sun-white hair flashing in the moonlight as he leaned over her on the pool chaise. Salt air and night flowers. She would get through this as sanely as possible. She had to.

She made her way carefully across the uneven driveway to the crumbling old adobe she called home. Yes, the wind always found its way into the house, even though she faithfully sealed the windows in plastic every winter. Yes, the hot water faucet on the kitchen sink never worked right. Yes, the ancient linoleum in the kitchen and bathroom curled up around the edges. She still felt embraced by its womb-like calm every time she came home.

She planned to stand a few piñon logs inside the tiny kiva fireplace in the corner of the living room, knowing that within minutes she would be sustained by its comforting warmth. She would turn on a small lamp, maybe light some candles, perhaps even dig around that dusty basket filled with old cassette tapes and retrieve some Billie Holiday, yes, or Julie London. She would bask in the voices of brokenhearted women singing smoky blues and mull over the messy closing of this chapter of her life.

The moon, so much brighter in the thin, high air of New Mexico than at the beach, lit the yard with a ghostly sheen, but the front doorway was dark; once in, she fumbled along the inside wall for the light switch. Chaos greeted her, but no stranger had come in looking for valuables—there was the TV, right next to the fireplace, the stereo comfortably nestled on top. No, the house felt like Michael, his rage visible in the disarray.

Broken dishes, overturned houseplants, and kitchen trash were strewn about the floor. Her basket of tapes and

CDs was upended, plastic cases smashed by an angry boot heel. She picked her way to the bedroom; the sheets had been yanked off the bed, her clothes ripped from the closet and dresser drawers and thrown about like puppy toys. Her eyes filled with tears. The back room, the one she had so painstakingly cleared of her things and refurnished for Michael when they married so he could have some space for himself, was empty.

What a fucking cliché. He was the one who'd left; did he expect her to be here when he came back? Too weary even for anger, she stuffed a few socks and things into the dresser drawer, glad to at least finally *know*. A box of photos spilled on the closet floor caught her eye: her wedding pictures. Their wedding. She stared at the pile for a long minute before scooping the pictures up and dumping them on the crumpled sheets on the floor. "Fine," she muttered, "fine. Let's just get the whole thing over with." Gathering up the sheets, the pictures tucked inside, Camelia headed back out the door, mindless of the detritus she crushed underfoot.

Several yards from the house, amid the grasses and bits of desert driftwood that had collected around the property, was a small fire pit ringed with rocks and a few abandoned cinder blocks. She had assembled it when she first moved to the little house, which was just far enough outside of town to make her feel she was really out in the desert, and she had celebrated her freedom from civilization with a bonfire every full moon. Eventually she abandoned the ritual; the fires became commonplace after a while, as did the beacon of the moon covering the mesa with silver, the wailing of the coyotes not so very far away, and the slithering bull snake that had taken up residence in the weeds and wild flowers alongside her driveway.

But tonight she was ready for what she could later call a perfect Santa Fe moment: a healing, she'd say, a cleansing signified by a ritual burning of all that was left of her marriage. More accurately, she just wanted to quickly erase the evidence of her poor judgment, the faster to get her life back on track.

The sheets were stubbornly inflammable; she dragged them back out of the pit, left them in the dirt, and ignited the pictures instead. She didn't need to see them one more time. She well remembered how she had marched through the entire proceeding with grim determination, a permanent smile pasted on her face, starkly aware even then that she was making a huge mistake. They curled and faded and disappeared. When the fire burned down to embers, she went back to the house, picked out everything else from the wreckage that might burn, and added it to the pile.

Another flare-up, more smoke and snapping and popping, and miscellaneous papers, an address book, mail addressed to Michael, even a file of papers she had brought home from work last week—it was last week, wasn't it?—all turned to ash.

"Take it all," Camelia told the fire quietly. "Just take it all and set me free."

Sitting on a broken cinder block, her eyes dry, she poked with a stick at what was left in the pit for a while. Aware now of the cold night air, she scraped at some dirt with her foot until she had enough to heap onto the remaining embers to extinguish them and then scuffed back into the house.

It was after two. Tucking a few logs into the kiva, she started another fire, this one tame enough to bring calm to the chaos in the house. Serious cleanup could wait; gathering up her pillows and blankets, she arranged herself in a nest on the wood floor of the living room. Still dressed in the T-shirt and jeans she had left Dos Palmas in, she watched the flames until her eyes slowly closed.

No marching band greeted her from the hills, no rooster welcomed the day; Thursday morning dawned clear but very cold. Camelia struggled out of her cocoon in the milky light, put more wood in the fireplace, and fell back asleep. By the time she woke again, the sun had warmed the day considerably, and she pushed herself to move. Hot coffee in hand, she idly wondered what she should do first. Change the locks, buy groceries, rearrange the furniture? How about get a job? She remembered the Tarot cards the man on the flight to Oaxaca had shown her last week. Change is internal, he had said; otherwise your problems follow you wherever you go. She might as well have thrown the cards in the air and let the Fates decide.

Still wrapped in a blanket, she stepped out on the front portal. The crisp air felt like a sharp knife in her sinuses after the soft humidity of the beach. When she had walked off the plane in Albuquerque last night she could feel the last drops of moisture being sucked out of her body by the dry, harsh air. If there was any need to remind herself she was back in the desert, that was enough.

She let the answering machine pick up the phone when it rang.

"Camelia, it's Melanie. Chris called me yesterday after you left; he's getting Nico on the plane today, he promised, and he'll be home tonight. Call me later." Her voice sounded tired. Camelia did not want to tell Melanie what she'd seen. Chris, so impersonal and self-protective. How much of himself he had given away in that little speech to her at Mel's. That bruise on Nico's cheek and the way

Chris had handled him, shoving him in the taxi like he was a bag of potatoes or a small, snarling dog.

Melanie. Nico. Chris. Eric. Michael. Too many people crowded inside her suddenly, and she longed for the solitude she always used to have in her little house out here on the llano under the clear blue bowl of New Mexico sky.

The February sun was bright. By noon, she would forsake her jacket and do just fine in a sweater. Or, just as likely, she would find herself running for cover while the temperature dropped and rain or sleet or hail hammered the hard-packed earth and surrounded her house with muck. It was the kind of weather that made people drive down the road one day and keep going, not stopping until they hit the end of the line, perhaps a quiet beach somewhere, a place where time stood still and the weather never changed. Shielding her eyes, she gazed out over the yard, taking in three different mountain ranges, and went in to refill her coffee cup.

She had always hated spring in Santa Fe. It wasn't really spring at all, it was just more winter, lasting too long, and then all of a sudden one day in June—or sometimes as early as April or as late as July—it would be summer, and the burning heat would erase any memory of the last week's snowstorm, the previous day's biting winds and overcast skies. Summers could be mild here, and sometimes they were positively lovely, with week after week of moderate heat and azure skies, blessedly lacking in the stifling humidity suffocating the rest of the country. Surprising little showers popped up in the afternoons to wash away the dust of the day, and the sunsets looked like the best efforts of Hollywood scene painters.

But somehow in the last few years even the weather had shifted, and Camelia was no longer entranced by Santa Fe's natural charms. Summers had been so dry, the only place to see bountiful gardens was on the walls of the Canyon Road art galleries; by September, her eyes felt seared. If it weren't for October, perhaps she'd have left Santa Fe long ago. In October, Santa Fe finally lived up to its hype, and she couldn't imagine ever being anywhere else on the planet. The memory of crisp blue skies, cottonwoods turning gold before her eyes, and the unmistakable way the light changed from summer's glaring brightness to the more diffuse halo of autumn might be all that kept her here year after year.

She sat at her kitchen table and looked around the little house, remembering her delight when she had first moved in; her own five-acre lot and low rent, plenty of authentic Santa Fe style even with its curling kitchen linoleum, an attentive but unobtrusive landlord. Neighbors were few and kept to themselves; she had lucked out with Claire, tucked quietly near the back end of the property and treasuring her own privacy. Isolation hadn't been her goal, but she thrived on the solitude even as she drove herself to search out a partner to share her tiny space with.

She had relished those big skies, loved to sit on her porch and watch the weather roll in season after season. The jagged horizon, the impossible sunsets and popcorn clouds were her own. She savored the idea of wide horizons leading to endless opportunities and rich possibilities. But today, everything was different. Today, the open sky made her nervous. She felt vulnerable and raw and ungrounded, the sky a vast hole she was in danger of shooting herself through, propelling herself out to space. If she moved into town, maybe she would feel a little more protected by the close-in houses and narrow streets, by the presence of others always nearby.

Ah, but moving took money, and to get money one must have a job. Even more than her marriage, and certainly more than the weather, this was really the crux of her problem at the moment, and she knew she couldn't ignore it forever. What kind of an employee goes out to lunch at Casa Abuelita's and never comes back? She hadn't exactly planned to leave her tedious position with the city's Arts Division, but it was unlikely she'd be able to claw her way back into it now. Like everything else in Santa Fe, her minor admin job processing grant requests seemed serene on the surface, but underneath it shifted and split apart in a continuous display of political plate tectonics.

Just before the Christmas holidays, a new boss had swept into Camelia's office and told her the department was being reorganized. "I just don't know if we're still going to be doing what you do here," she had told Camelia, looking her straight in the eye. You have no idea what I do here, Camelia thought at the time. "I'm sure we'll be able to find something for you to do, but in the meantime, don't kill yourself trying to finish up whatever you're working on. It's not really going to matter in the long run anyway." With a dismissive wave toward Camelia's desk, she swept back out, leaving the door open behind her.

"What does that mean?" Claire had met her for a margarita after work on the heated outdoor balcony of the Ore House that same day.

"I haven't the slightest idea." Camelia's eyes roamed over the Plaza's meager holiday decorations. "It doesn't matter to me; I certainly don't care if individual artists get grants from the city or not. But it is a job, and a fairly decent one pay-wise anyway. I don't know what I'll do if they squeeze me out."

She was sure if she called in to work today they'd say, "Camelia who?" Nobody bothered her there; nobody seemed to pay much attention to her at all. She wasn't invited to the casual meetings over lunch in pricey downtown restaurants; she found out about after-hours meetings in her own office when she came in the next morning and cleared away coffee cups and wads of crumpled notebook paper from her desk. She should have started looking for a new job months ago. Along with everything else she should have done.

Leaving her coffee cup in the sink, she swept some of the litter around her to the corners of the little kitchen, pulled on her boots and jacket, and left the house. She would shop, she would eat somewhere, she would take care of things later.

The next morning, Camelia dutifully opened the *Santa Fe Daily* to the classifieds and made some desultory red circles around a few likely possibilities. She had started to clean her house yesterday afternoon and instead ended up napping in front of the fireplace well into the night. Today her thoughts kept returning to Dos Palmas. By noon, the newspaper was covered with doodles and coffee rings; she hadn't made one call. The red light on her answering machine blinked ceaselessly; Melanie had left two more messages, none of which she returned.

She finally roused herself long enough to clean up the mess in the bathroom—clotted shampoo in the tub, broken glass in the sink—and took a hot shower. Wrapping herself up in her blankets on the floor in front of the fireplace, as she had the day before, she watched the fire until she dozed off. New sheets sat unopened in a bag in her bedroom. As she drifted into a late afternoon nap, she vowed to stay there on the floor until she had a good reason to get up again.

14 The Land of Entrapment

The endless night of the highway finally gave way to distant city lights spread out before him in the chilly darkness. Cresting the northernmost edge of La Bajada, Eric became aware of two important points. February meant winter up here; he was freezing in shorts and flip-flops and had been for hours. And he had no idea where he would go once he hit the Santa Fe exits. He had been driving since dawn on Wednesday, and now he was pretty sure it was close to midnight on Friday night. It wasn't the first time in his life he had made a hasty and unplanned departure, but a sudden panic began to bubble in his chest. A realtor's billboard brightly proclaimed, "Welcome Home!"

"First things first," he said loudly, switching off the tinny truck radio as he turned into the rest-stop parking lot, only minutes away from the city he had left a few years ago with little more than he had with him right now. He dug around under the seats until he located the remains of his old Santa Fe wardrobe and headed into the men's room. Shaking out sand and the dried carcasses of a few bugs from the wad of clothing, he pulled on a pair of jeans, a threadbare flannel shirt, a wool sweater, and an ancient denim jacket over the old blue T-shirt he had been wearing since the night at the Hotel Paloma Blanca's restaurant when Camelia, who had strolled so carelessly into his heart only days before, moved into his soul as well.

She was all he could think of as he had driven away for the last time from Dos Palmas, his neighbor's chickens scattering in the alley, a lone beach towel still hanging over the railing of his portal. It wasn't her face he saw as he drove, but the intensity in her eyes when she looked at him, as though she were drilling a hole right through the layers of bullshit and alcohol and excuses until she could see whatever was left of the man he had once thought he could be, whatever tiny spark might still be there, salvageable. He thought of her reckless determination to match him drink for drink that first day, saw in her a drive toward an obliteration she didn't deserve. That, perhaps more than anything else, frightened him enough to quit drinking altogether.

And he saw the trembling of her hand as she looked away from him, talking about her husband and her broken heart; he saw the quickness of her smile when, caught off guard, her armor fell away. His hands in her hair, his tongue in her mouth; he had been drawn into a warm red whirling storm he wished he could live inside of, embraced, forever.

He had driven fast that morning, kicking up clouds of road dust as he passed through little villages up along the coastal highway. Finally turning inland at Jalisco, he headed straight north through Guadalajara and a succession of villages and cities and long stretches of wild emptiness with little awareness of the countryside he had seen only once before. He had tried unsuccessfully to nap in the bed of his pickup for a few hours; by the time he crossed through Durango into Chihuahua yesterday afternoon, with at least another day of driving ahead of him, he gave in. Stumbling upon a tiny motel that was, if not in the middle of nowhere, then certainly close to it, he sank like a stone into the flimsy mattress, its ticking barely concealed by a sheet washed too many times. Sleep had been elusive those last few days at the beach before he left. By the time he stopped driving, sheer exhaustion took him down far enough to stop running.

And now, tonight, he rubbed the warmth into his hands as he stood in front of what passed for a mirror at the Santa Fe rest stop, a polished sheet of metal that only gave the illusion of reflection. Still, he could see the worn-out look around his eyes and the slack in his jawline. He knew he was more than just tired from his marathon drive; he looked used up, broken, lost. He hurried back to his truck and pulled out onto the highway with new determination. Melanie. He'd go to Melanie's.

With a quiet certainty, he knew there was someone else he needed to find before he looked for Camelia, and that was his own son, his boy Zane. Eric had never given a thought to having a child before the day Shelley announced she was pregnant, and he had tried to do what he thought was right. He married her, even though their relationship was more off-again than on; how could he have known that wasn't what she wanted after all?

He had gone to work for a cabinetmaker in a stuffy warehouse-turned-factory in the barrio off Agua Fria to keep a paycheck coming in; he went through the childbirth classes and held her for hours when she went into labor. He now remembered the moment he first held his son, how his feelings had sent him tumbling, electrified. Then she took the baby in her own arms, and that was it; the door to her heart closed with finality, and he often felt like an interloper in his own house. It didn't take much of a leap to one day find himself driving past his own street and onto the southbound lanes of the interstate without ever looking back.

Gringo loco, they called him on the beach; oh, how right they were, they had no idea. He turned the radio on as loud as it would go. He knew Melanie and Chris lived somewhere on the east side of town in the historic district, marked by narrow, winding lanes and low adobe houses, where sprawling estates owned by out-of-towners bumped up against crumbling casitas stubbornly held by single families for generations.

Martinez Liquorette, an anomaly on an otherwise solidly residential street, was still open; he turned the truck into the store's single parking space to see if he could find a phone book and the Sullivans' address. A liquor store, wasn't that just exactly the place he needed to be right now? The sleepy clerk glanced his way and continued his phone conversation for several minutes. Eric pulled out his cigarettes and tapped the lighter on the counter, looking around the store with mild fascination at the sheer variety of processed, commercial booze. His heart began to beat loudly in his ears, and he willed the sight of all those glittering bottles to disappear.

"Hold on just a second, babe," the clerk said into the phone. "What you want, man?"

"Hey, just a phone book, nothing serious." The young man pulled out a ragged book from under the counter, tossed it across to Eric, and returned to his conversation. Oh yeah, the City Indifferent, Eric remembered as he ripped out the page he needed. "Adios," he called out as he left. He could hear the bolt slide across the door behind him.

He zigzagged quickly through the neighborhoods, looking for familiar street names, and thought of Melanie, whose care and support had held him together when he'd first landed in Dos Palmas. Now she was stuck with her two self-absorbed teenagers in the muck of a messy Santa Fe winter while Chris played swinging bachelor at the beach. He remembered when Nico had been a genial, outgoing child and how he had turned sullen adolescent overnight. Chris's usual friendly demeanor had gone sour; Melanie had become vague and listless.

Eric never told Chris that during one of his solitary moonlit walks a year or so ago he had come upon them packing up. He could see the whole family through the front windows of their brightly lit house, and without thinking he stood on the beach in the darkness and watched. He still remembered how electric that night had seemed. Melanie, crying angrily and throwing things in suitcases. Rayne, perhaps twelve or thirteen, so quiet and frozen in space she almost disappeared. Nico and Chris, huddled in the kitchen.

It was one of the few events in Dos Palmas he could recall now that was not met with the customary gossip before the next tide. On the contrary, the entire village had remained unusually tight-lipped about the episode. He sometimes wondered if it had really happened at all.

There were few other cars on the streets at this hour. He remembered how he had once loved the little town in its quiet darkness. The squat, mud-colored houses, the streets with no names, the sense of timelessness that had first drawn him to Santa Fe so many years before seemed acute in the nether hours. He rolled down the window, breathing in the cold air and the mellow scent of burning piñon from a wood stove somewhere in the neighborhood. Home.

The ringing phone late Friday night startled Camelia from a deep sleep, and it took her some moments to place not only where the phone was but where she was. The fire had burned down to nothing hours ago, and the house was cold. She had been wrapped up in her blankets on the floor, still dressed in jeans and a coral-colored turtleneck, since late afternoon; now her back and legs felt stiff as rusted wire. She stumbled to the kitchen light switch and squinted against the glare to locate the phone.

"Camelia, it's Chris," she heard before she even said hello. His voice was thick, as though he or the phone itself was submerged in murky water. "I need you to go to Melanie. Go *now*. I'll be there sometime tomorrow. Don't leave her until I get there. Promise me. Promise me you won't leave her side until I get there!" The panic in his voice shot through her with the precision of an arrow.

"Yes, of course, I promise. What's going on?" Her own voice sounded foreign to her, laced through with fear and dread.

He screamed at her to "just go!" and hung up. Camelia struggled into her boots and grabbed her coat from the rack by the front door. She ran out, then back in again, picked up her purse from the kitchen table, dug about madly for her keys.

"Come on, come on, come on, you stupid piece of junk!" she screamed at the car, pounding the steering wheel when it failed to start after several trics. Finally the engine caught and she pulled out of her driveway, the noise surreal in the cold, quiet darkness.

I promise: it was a phrase that had become a minefield for her lately. She had promised Melanie she would bring Nico home, but she got on the plane without him. She had said it to Michael, too, on their wedding day, but that didn't stop her from sleeping with Eric. Now she said it to

Chris. And what had she promised? She had no idea. Her teeth chattered, though not from the cold. The clanky heater was working fine, and the car was already stifling. Her entire body shivered, and she struggled to keep her hands still enough on the wheel to navigate the perils of Cerrillos Road, the main thoroughfare from the south end of town and a daily test of her own driving acumen.

Camelia gritted her teeth and hugged the right lane. Melanie's messages on her answering machine gave no indication of anything being wrong, certainly nothing so serious as to require—what, a witness, a guardian, a nurse? Nico had arrived home last night as planned; as far as she was concerned, the rest of it was their business, not hers. Sweat broke out on her scalp and dripped down the back of her neck. She drove slowly as other drivers cruised through red lights with abandon, changed lanes from side to side without warning, made left turns from right-hand lanes. No matter that it was near midnight; it was Friday, and all of Santa Fe seemed to be out late and drunk.

She changed lanes twice for police cars pulling over offenders; some traffic was backed up onto the road from the drive-through lane at a liquor store, but she got around that pretty quickly. Then she watched a fender bender happen in front of her near the country-western bar, but, mercifully, both drivers pulled into the parking lot before flinging their doors open and lunging at each other.

Eventually the speed, the noise, and the lights of the busy boulevard all choked themselves down into a quiet two-lane road lined with small businesses, their lights off, their tiny parking lots empty. Camelia felt her racing heart slow as the traffic disappeared. She had never hated the long drive into the city as much as she did tonight, and she resolved to move closer into town as soon as she could, maybe even into the quiet neighborhood where Melanie lived, if she could find a way to afford it. She turned down Acequia Madre and peered into the darkness so she wouldn't miss the narrow street where the Sullivans lived.

Eric turned a corner onto a rough, unlit lane, and his contentment vanished. The flashing blue lights of several police cars threw alien moonbeams on the Sullivan house. Once more he found himself watching through the windows at a family crisis. This time, mezcal did not fuse his feet to ground. He ran up the front walk and let himself in.

The house was dark save for one small lamp in the living room. Melanie was on the couch, silent as ice, her eyes two orbs of glass. Half a dozen cops milled around the room speaking in low tones, the screech from their walkie-talkies punctuating the heavy air. They barely glanced at him. The phone rang several times, stopped, then started again. What the fuck? His head cleared with the finality of a knife strike.

"You guys all done here or what?" he said to a policeman standing near the door.

"Who are you?" There was a hostility in the cop's voice that startled Eric.

"Family friend," he answered, caution holding his tongue in the sudden silence as the phone stopped ringing.

The cop looked him over a moment, glanced at Melanie, then signaled the other men with a nod of his chin, pursing his lips toward the door. A short conversation followed, and within minutes, the room was empty save for Melanie and Eric. The blaring lights from the driveway were turned off, and the police cars sped away, their tires crunching on the dirt road. Melanie remained silent.

"Let me get a fire going; it's kind of chilly in here," he said to her, pulling a worn Mexican blanket from the couch over her shoulders. She didn't move. He went to the fireplace and busied himself with kindling and newspapers. His hands felt brittle and clumsy. A cold, wet fear gripped him inside and slithered like a snake through his limbs, contracting every muscle in his body. His jaw clenched so tightly his teeth hurt, and he waited until the fire was going before he turned to Melanie again.

"Nico's dead," she whispered. "Shot. Guy down the street thought he was breaking into his house."

The phone started to ring again. He forced himself to breathe. A wave of dread washed over him, filling his throat with bile and leaving a sour taste in his mouth.

"The cops?"

She shook her head. "The owner. Just moved in last month. From California, I think. Does something with computers. Shot him first, then called the cops." Her voice trickled to a stop; she sighed loudly and pulled the blanket tighter around her shoulders.

"Where's Rayne?" he asked, sharply aware of the girl's absence.

"Gone."

His throat filled up again, and for a moment he thought he might choke or drown. "Gone? What does that mean?"

"She left last month, day she turned fifteen. I thought Chris told you." Her eyes shifted in and out of focus. "What are you doing here, Eric?"

Eric listened to the fire crackle and spit and wondered how much loss anyone had to endure before being allowed to simply give up. He placed his hands on hers to stop them from unraveling the already fraying edges of the blanket.

"Where did she go?" He said it as carefully as he could.

"Ireland." Melanie put her head back on the sofa and shut her eyes.

"*Ireland?*"

"Distant cousins. She called Chris in Mexico from the airport in New York just before she got on a plane. We called them; she's there, she's fine, they had no idea she was a runaway. She refuses to speak to us."

In a queer way, the talk of Rayne seemed to revive Melanie, if only for a moment. It also kept Eric from fully embracing the words he had heard when he first came in. Nico's dead. Did she really say that?

"At first, I couldn't figure out how she managed to get so many of her things packed and out of the house without my noticing. When Chris called me from the hotel, I didn't even realize she was gone. But the truth is, I had been so mired in Nico's constant problems she could have painted her room purple and had a family of prairie dogs living under her bed and I would never have known."

The phone, which had stopped, started to ring again, and she threw a small pillow at it, knocking it off the end table and silencing it.

"Chris'll be home soon," she said, holding her hands out to the fire like a small child. "He'll know what to do. Nico was just hanging out with his friends. He wasn't breaking in. He didn't have a gun. He was on his way home, just cutting through the guy's yard; I'm sure of it." She stared dully at the fire.

Eric stood silently. Why did life always have to be about losing? It didn't seem fair somehow that as soon as you thought you'd figured things out, you got upended and had to start all over. The disconnection he had so carefully cultivated during his years in Dos Palmas was gone, first chipped away by a tender woman and now shattered by a bullet in the cold winter night. He felt himself sinking to the earth from a great height, his feet now and forever firmly on the ground.

"I'll make some coffee," he said finally, heading into the kitchen.

Camelia rushed up the front walk and pushed opened the door. Melanie was sitting on the couch in front of a blazing fireplace. Eric walked in from the kitchen, two cups of coffee in his hands.

"Close the door, it's cold," Melanie said quietly, her gaze locked on the fire.

"Sorry, I—Chris called, he told me to come over. What's going on?" Camelia hurried over to Melanie, but Melanie closed her eyes and turned away. Camelia felt her stomach go to ice. She looked up. "Eric?" He put the coffee cups down on the table in front of the couch and motioned to her to follow him to the doorway.

"It's Nico. Shot. Down the street. It's a big fucking mess." He took her hands as she started to sway.

Shot?

How could someone use that word in any sort of ordinary sentence?

"Come into the kitchen with me; I'll get you a cup of coffee," he said, leading her toward a chair at the kitchen table. He quickly repeated Melanie's sketchy details and handed her a steaming cup as she sat in silence.

"Coffee. Of course," she said finally, both hands shaking as she laced them around the warm cup. How had he gotten here so fast, all the way from the beach, if all this craziness had just happened and Chris was still in Mexico when he called her half an hour ago? She stared at the coils of steam rising from the coffee, trying to make sense of everything. And then she remembered Chuey, *el taxista*, talking about how the *gringo loco* had failed to show up at the shake shack two days ago.

"Oh my God. Did you *drive* here?" He raised his eyes to hers; she couldn't breathe.

"Good coffee, Eric," Melanie said from the other room.

"Oh, Melanie, I just don't know what to say." Camelia hurried into the living room, took Melanie's ice-cold hand into hers, and rubbed it. "I'm so sorry about Nico. What can I do?"

"I know why you're here," Melanie responded after a minute, "but I have yet to find out what the hell he's doing here. I had just returned from a fascinating visit to the morgue, and he walked in the door a little while ago and chased all the cops away."

"What can I tell you, Melanie? I woke up one morning and decided I didn't feel like opening Mel's, and instead I drove to Santa Fe," Eric said as he lit a cigarette. "Hardly a surprise; it's not like I haven't ever done anything like that before."

Camelia noted the stubble on his cheeks, the clothes that might have been rifled from a Salvation Army bin. Her heart beat in her ears; he didn't look at her.

"That's why we call it the Land of Entrapment. It's impossible to leave for very long." Melanie sighed and closed her eyes.

Nico. Eric. Melanie. Camelia's head felt too full. She went back into the kitchen for her coffee and returned with a bottle of Jameson she had spotted on the cluttered counter. She poured a generous shot in Melanie's cup and a bit for herself; Eric placed his hand flat over his cup but said nothing.

Surrounded by scratchy Mexican blankets and pillows, they sat huddled together through the night as the fire's glow soothed the bleak room, saying little. Once or twice Camelia felt herself doze off but jerked herself awake again. Eric brought in firewood, poked at the burning logs, lit cigarettes, and stared at the flames. Melanie, holding Camelia's hand, sometimes hummed tunelessly but never cried. Camelia wondered how long she would last, strung out on shock and caffeine, whiskey and tobacco.

Around dawn, Eric got up to place another log on the fire, and when he sat back down, Melanie was sound asleep. He tucked a blanket around her, stood, and stretched. Camelia also rose, mindful not to wake Melanie, and looked at him. She felt her heart open in a way she almost couldn't bear; he folded his arms around her, buried his face in her hair. They stood in front of the fireplace and cried.

"I can't even begin to wonder what Chris must feel right now," Eric said, taking her hand and walking into the kitchen. He rinsed the coffeepot and refilled it. "I just know how I feel, and I only hope I can get through the next day or so for their sakes." He wiped at his eyes with his sleeve. "It's just unbelievable. He was just a kid."

"How can the world just spin off its axis like that?" Camelia whispered. "How can everything fall apart so fast?" She thought of Nico sitting at the bar of the Paloma Blanca and felt her stomach contract. She gripped the edge of the table until her fingers turned white.

"I can say this," Eric answered, his eyes on the dripping coffee, his back to Camelia. "It's one thing to leave your family behind and just keep driving to the ends of the earth. You know what you're doing, even while you're doing it, and you keep going anyway and drink yourself into believing it's OK." He rubbed a finger against the counter tile, then swiped his hand across his eyes.

"It's another thing entirely to go to bed with your heart intact and wake up to a cop telling you your kid is dead."

15 The Sleep of the Dead

"I'm going to get a little air," Eric whispered to Camelia. She sat in the kitchen with him, her head resting on her arms on the table, her eyes closed. Time had stood still through the long night; he wondered if he would ever sleep again. How could she still be so beautiful, he thought, even after all this? How could she even be here, how could he have held her and cried with her, how could he have felt her warm tears on his neck and not simply fallen into a crack in the earth or blasted apart into a million pieces?

He stood on the front portal in the chilly darkness and watched the sky lighten, then picked up the morning paper from the walk and glanced at the headline before heading back inside. And then he stopped and looked at it again and waited for it to make sense.

"ANGLO NEWCOMER KILLS HISPANIC TEEN."

The frigid morning air did not deter him; he read the entire story twice before going back inside. On the couch, Melanie still slept deeply. He poked at the fire and was tempted to toss the paper in. Instead, he slid it onto the kitchen table in front of Camelia, his hand on her back, and whispered, "Can you explain this to me?"

"'I heard a male voice saying something in Spanish outside the front window,'" she read quietly. "'It sounded like there was more than one person, but I couldn't understand what they were saying. I was afraid they might have guns. I thought they were breaking in.'"

He felt the pure calm of the unrested, even as he could see the day in front of him, and many, many more days ahead, pull away from his grasp and spin out of reach.

"'This is just the sort of thing we can expect to happen when people come here from someplace else and build big houses and live behind gates and don't bother to try to fit in,' the mayor, who was contacted at home after the shooting, said. 'I wouldn't be surprised if there was some kind of angry response from the community.'" Camelia sighed and pushed the paper aside.

Movement outside the window caught Eric's attention. He watched a small old woman clothed in black hesitantly approach the house; she deposited a humble bunch of flowers at the bottom of the front walk, made the sign of the cross, and walked away. His eyes burned. It was a vision he might have seen in Santa Fe many years ago, or perhaps in the mountain villages above Dos Palmas, but today he knew there was no one out there but a hardy raven poking around the yard for an early breakfast.

Crime in Santa Fe was mostly crime of opportunity, Chris had told him once years ago. It was small-time and kind of stupid, and it preyed on people who did stupid things, like leaving the keys in the car or not bothering to lock up the house when they went to work. "Some of the bad guys have guns, but they mostly use them on each other. Maybe it's a kind of natural selection," Chris had said, and they'd laughed.

Eric wasn't sure where Nico fit into that equation.

Camelia picked up the paper again and glanced through the story. "I can't fucking believe this. I just can't." She put her head in her arms on the table; he could see her shoulders shake as she wept.

Melanie hadn't stirred. Eric remembered that night in Dos Palmas, Camelia talking about the sleep of the dead, and he felt his chest constrict. Mezcal and lime, cigarette smoke, citronella. The whispering of palm fronds, waves on the beach. The rosy turtleneck she wore today brought fire to her cheeks, and he stood behind her for several minutes. Eventually he turned away and flicked on the small TV on the kitchen counter, just to remind himself that the rest of the world was still normal. He watched an old Road Runner cartoon for a few minutes before switching to a local newscast.

"It's seven fifteen and 32 degrees here in Albuquerque on this bright but chilly Saturday morning," began the chipper anchorwoman. "In Santa Fe last night, a Hispanic teenager who may or may not have been breaking into a house was apparently shot dead by the Anglo homeowner in what some members of the community are calling a racially motivated killing. Community activists have planned a rally for ten o'clock this morning on the Plaza to protest the lenient treatment of the homeowner, who was not arrested after claiming self-defense.

"Santa Fe's mayor, who has indicated his displeasure with the police department several times in the past year, is planning a private meeting with the chief of police. That meeting has yet to be scheduled. In addition, the mayor has repeated his recent call for an investigation into the approval of recent real-estate development applications, indicating he wants to know how many approvals have gone to real estate companies operated from out of state. In other news, Albuquerque city commissioners wrapped up preparations yesterday for their upcoming debate on the rezoning of the downtown corridor . . ."

"But he's an *Anglo*, dammit! He's a white kid, and they know it!" Eric reeled, switching off the TV with a violence that almost knocked it off the counter. Camelia jumped, startled. "She went to the morgue; she identified him. What part of *Sullivan* don't they understand?"

He paced around the kitchen, momentarily unable to collect his thoughts. It was as though Santa Fe itself—not just Chris and Melanie's family—had had the rug pulled out from under it. He remembered Santa Fe as a town just small enough to take a single innocuous event and turn it into a collective obsession, but he would much rather have watched it from the sidelines.

"There's something strange about all this," Camelia said slowly. "I mean, first of all, how could they make that kind of mistake—and get it in the paper so quickly, too? Wouldn't the reporter have gotten the records from the morgue or maybe even been there at the same time? I've never really understood how they get their news, if the reporters follow the cops around or the cops call the reporters. Or maybe the cops didn't even tell the reporter everything that happened." She stared at the newspaper story again.

"These people they're quoting, I've seen their names in the paper, letters to the editor, that kind of thing," she continued. "They complain about how there's been this influx of wealthy Anglos turning Santa Fe into an adobe Disneyland, which of course they're right about. There's been all kinds of fallout from the sort of tourism department version of Santa Fe, and I suppose we're all guilty on one level, believing in 'Santa Fe Style' instead of, you know, the real thing. But what's this about a rally? How could someone plan a rally for ten o'clock this morning—a Saturday—when this whole thing just happened a few hours ago, *and* tell the television station in time to get it on the early morning news?" She looked at Eric.

He hadn't been on the beach all that long; well before he'd left it behind, Santa Fe's complex social issues had been visible all around him. The big houses and the trailer parks, the glittery art scene and the homeless teenagers hanging out on the Plaza, the heroin and the poverty and the women gone missing. That's why he rarely paid attention to Chris's endless attempts to develop Dos Palmas while also trying to circumvent Mexican politics. Strategizing and layered conflicts gave Eric a headache; he could taste the raw smoke of mezcal suddenly at the back of his throat and knew why it had been his favored escape.

"Maybe someone was just waiting for something to happen to give them an excuse for this rally," he said after a moment.

"It's not like it's impossible." She turned back to the paper. "I just don't understand. What does all this have to do with Nico?"

He considered. "OK, here's what we're going to do," he said finally, stepping into the living room to find the phone Melanie had buried under a pillow last night. Just as he connected it, the phone rang.

"Sullivans'." He headed back into the kitchen, his eyes on Camelia.

"Federico Ulibarri, *Santa Fe Daily*. Sorry to bother you, I know this must be a difficult time for you."

So the reporter had called him; maybe this wasn't going to be too hard after all.

"Oh, are you the *estúpido* responsible for this insane headline?" He tried to keep his voice low.

"Like I say, I'm sorry to bother you, but I'm just calling to verify the boy's age. The cops are saying maybe seventeen; if he's a minor, we won't be printing his name, but I do need to verify it just the same, for my files, for future reference, you know?"

"*Maybe* seventeen? You didn't get any facts from the cops, that's obvious. So verify this, asshole. He's Anglo, *comprende*? Maybe he was at that guy's house, maybe the guy had a right to shoot if he thought he was in danger, but let's not make a race war out of this. This is some big, ugly mess, but it's not Anglo against Hispanic, you got me?"

Once again there was silence at the other end of the phone. Eric rubbed his eyes and tried to slow his breathing. "You still there, *cabrón*?"

Finally a long, slow whistle came from the reporter.

"*¡Hijole!* The kid's an Anglo? But that's not what . . ." He stopped talking suddenly, and Eric felt the fine hairs on the back of his neck rise up.

"So much for your big story, huh?" Eric said quietly. "Call that *borracho* mayor and straighten this mess out, or I'm coming down there to straighten you out. Got it?" He tossed the phone onto the counter; Melanie stirred slightly but didn't awaken. "What will we tell her?" Camelia said.

"Christ, I don't know." Eric paced around, running his fingers along the cobalt blue tiles that lined the counter. "This stinks. That guy, the way he sounded—someone gave him the wrong information, maybe on purpose, I don't know why. How can we hide it from her?"

"Do you think we should? I mean, it's just unbelievable. How can we not?"

Eric rinsed his coffee cup. He was starving. "It'll be hours before Chris gets here."

She spread her hands across the newspaper as if willing the story to disappear underneath them.

Eric sighed deeply. He had gone to extreme lengths in his life to avoid confrontation, but those days were over. "I'll go to the newspaper or maybe the mayor's office and try to talk some sense into somebody. Can you stay here with Melanie?"

"Of course. I promised Chris I wouldn't leave her side until he got here." Camelia's voice broke; a surreal combination of grief, panic, and desire threatened to suffocate him. He struggled to breathe. Oh, to be on the beach cutting oranges right now. Oh, to sink into the oblivion of mezcal, the ignorance of the sedated.

"I won't be gone long," he said, wrapping his arms around her, wishing they were wings that could take them both far away. "Just sit tight. Don't answer the phone, don't open the door, close the curtains, and keep the fire going."

"What should I tell her? Eric, she needs to know."

"You can show her the paper if she asks, or better yet, just leave it out here in the kitchen for now. We'll have to tell Chris, that's for sure. Maybe I can try to catch the mayor before this stupid rally. Which I guess I better go to as well. Shit. Look, I'll come back right after I go to the Plaza and let you know what's going on. Maybe you can just cocoon in here for a while."

Camelia smiled. "Oh, I've been getting pretty good at cocooning; it's all I've done since I got back."

He framed her face in his hands for a moment. "I never would have gotten through this night without you here," he whispered in her ear, the scent of piñon smoke in her hair driving straight through to his soul. "I'll be back as soon as I can."

Once Eric left, Camelia carefully added the last log to the fire and peered out the front window. Spotting the forlorn remains of a nearly depleted woodpile on the portal, she headed outside. Her hands were dry and chapped, and her mouth felt like she had been chewing on styrofoam. She flinched at the sound of a raven squawking overhead as she went back inside, arms awkwardly loaded. One more cup of coffee would surely put her over the edge. She couldn't remember when she had last eaten.

She grabbed the poker and made a few stabs at the dying fire. Out of the corner of her eye, the sight of a school notebook stopped her short. "American History" it said on the cover, nearly obliterated by doodles and scribbles and heavily inked names of rock bands and florid four-letter words. Perhaps it had been hastily dropped on the front table just yesterday afternoon. She felt as though the floor were falling out from underneath her even as she continued to stand on it.

"Let's get that fire going, huh? This'll work fine," Melanie said from behind her, and her frail, childlike hand snaked onto the table and grabbed the notebook before Camelia had a chance to breathe. Melanie tossed the notebook into the fireplace and poked at it a few times until a few loose pages finally caught.

"There's got to be a few more things around here we can use to get this baby going again. I always wind up letting the damn thing go out because I fall asleep on the couch, instead of feeding it consistently the way I should before going to bed, like a real grown-up would do. Let's see. I highly doubt there are any more notebooks around; I didn't think he had any at all, considering how little time he actually spent at school anyway. But there's got to be something."

Camelia stood quietly at alert, watching Melanie with growing dread. Her dark curls were smashed flat against her head, her red eyes, puffy. She wore faded black leggings with oversized, mismatched socks, a collection of sweaters and blankets layered around her shoulders.

"There's got to be more paper in the house, I'm sure of it. Wait, I know; don't move, Camelia, I'll take care of this right away." She scurried out of the room, her wool socks scuffling along the brick floors, and raced up the narrow staircase to the second floor.

Her hand shaking, Camelia poked at the fire again and listened to Melanie knocking things over upstairs. She should go up there, she knew. She should sit with Melanie and try to calm her. She should throw that damn newspaper in the fire. She should do something besides stand here feeling useless. Melanie, muttering, appeared at her side, arms loaded with spiral notebooks, notepads, and file folders. An unexpected anger ignited inside Camelia.

"What the fuck is all this? What are you going to do, burn the whole house down? Burn everything of his as if it doesn't exist, as if he never existed? Do you think that's going to set you free?"

Melanie sat down abruptly, scattering papers around her.

"Oh, shit, Melanie. I'm so sorry." Camelia joined her on the couch, suddenly worn out. She ran her fingers through her tangled hair. "I don't know how to even begin to help you."

"I don't know what I feel," Melanie said. "I'm crazy one minute and perfectly clear the next. I want to blame myself, and then I think, that's stupid, I didn't shoot him, I didn't tell him to go out there acting like a goddamned gangster all the time. I want to blame Chris, and then I think, well, yes, I do blame Chris. I think, if he had been here this wouldn't have happened. Then I think, what difference could he have made, what difference could either of us have made?

"And then I think that man moved in down the street for no other reason than to be awakened by the sounds of a bunch of shadowy kids in his yard; he moved to Santa Fe for no other reason than at that split second to reach for a gun when any normal person would have just called 9-1-1. He was born and lived in California and learned something about computers for the sole reason that he would eventually move to Santa Fe and set up an office in his house and keep a gun under his bed because of something he read in the papers about racial tension." She absently picked a piece of lint off her sleeve. "I could use some coffee."

The fire now forgotten, Melanie walked directly to the kitchen and emptied the cold coffeepot into the sink. Camelia, still on the couch, felt her heartbeat suddenly accelerate, but she couldn't make herself move. Just leave it out on the table, Eric had said about the newspaper. What did he know about anything, anyway? He was leaving. He had walked out of this house and away from all this grief and terror as surely as he had driven away from his family. For all she knew, he could have just gotten into his truck this morning and driven straight back to Dos Palmas.

She could hear Melanie putting cups into the sink, pouring coffee beans into the grinder. The newspaper, the newspaper was on the kitchen table. Camelia rose to gather the stray papers and notebooks Melanie had dropped and formed them into a loose assemblage, hoping to create some kind of order in this tiny universe to stave off for a minute or two the chaos she knew awaited.

"Camelia?" Melanie stood in the kitchen doorway, her voice as normal as a brown-bag lunch, a ticking clock, an afternoon nap.

Camelia turned to face her, a deep heat burning in her gut.

"Milk? Sugar?" Melanie remained motionless, a look of expectation on her wan face.

"Yes, fine, both, lots." Camelia followed her friend into the kitchen. Melanie had gone to the sink, her back to Camelia, and rinsed off some spoons. The aroma of fresh coffee filled the room.

"Camelia?"

"Right here, Melanie. Here, let me do that." She tried to take a spoon from her hands, but Melanie didn't let go.

"Why don't you check the fire, OK? You can use that newspaper if you like. Perhaps I will hold onto his other things for a little while, as you said. Burning *them* isn't really the point anyway, is it?"

She turned away from Camelia and reached for some clean mugs in the cupboard. Camelia tried to breathe.

"Go ahead, throw the paper into the fire. I don't know why we even get that rag here anymore. I never bother to read it. 'If it's news, it's news to us'—isn't that their motto? Here's your coffee. I'll just set it on the table. Would you please go throw that thing in the fire for me, or should I do it?"

"Right, of course, let's see if we can't get a little inferno going here anyway," Camelia said, grabbing the paper as she left the room. She pulled it apart quickly, savagely shoving pages into the still-hot embers.

"You might want to see if you can get that thing out of there soon." Melanie stood at her shoulder and pointed at the wire spiral from Nico's notebook, still attached to some slightly charred paper and the cardboard cover. She went back into the kitchen; Camelia took the poker and stood at the fireplace for several minutes, hot tears slowly making their way down her cheeks.

16 Like a House on a Fault Line

A hundred-dollar bill waved in front of the cabdriver, in the process of declining, guaranteed Chris quick passage from the airport in Albuquerque to his house in Santa Fe. He sat back in the taxi and covered his face with his hands. I made it this far, he told himself. I'll be home in an hour. I'm relatively sober. I can handle this. He wanted to cry, to vomit, to scream. He wanted to sleep, to sleep and never wake up. He wanted to crash along I-25 in such a blaze of fury that his blackened body would be irretrievable, mere ash floating to the sky. He wanted to drink—the most expensive tequila or the cheapest, rawest mezcal, or just perhaps some drain cleaner, to fill his gut with poison and stop the pain forever.

The call had come late last night, but he hadn't been able to get out of Dos Palmas until dawn. Ángel, the lone pilot who flew back and forth between the coast and the city of Oaxaca every day, had vanished for the night; Chris checked his little shack and every bar in three nearby villages several times over before reluctantly retreating to the Paloma Blanca to figure out his options. The young Brazilian dancer with the fourteen tiny earrings cascading along one earlobe had long since left his casita, leaving behind only the scent of honey and vanilla. At least he had been able to reach Camelia; at least one thing had gone right.

He had sat alone at the darkened bar with a citronella candle and a small glass of mezcal and felt himself collapse from the inside, the way old buildings do when they are purposely destroyed. Implosion, they call it. There is always that moment after the detonation—a breath, a respite—when the building seems to withstand the inner shock. Then it slowly caves in from the inside while the exterior remains unmoving. An instant later, the whole thing crashes straight down into the ground, a huge cloud of dust and smoke and debris rising from its foundations.

His son was dead. Shot, if he'd heard it right, by a neighbor who thought Nico was a burglar. His wife was at home, alone. He was stuck on the southern coast of Mexico. His old VW van would never make it to the airport in Ciudad Oaxaca, he knew. It had barely made it back down from the mountains after Carnaval, although he made sure none of his passengers knew just how tenuous the vehicle was. Driving to Oaxaca would take all night in a steady upward climb, but even if he managed to keep it running the whole way, the altitude would probably kill it.

And so he had walked on the beach for a long time, stood in the cool wash of the tide, stared out at the fading halo of the waning moon as it danced on the waves. He could no longer think of what he should do next or what might be happening back home. He felt only the void. He knew that he was alone, that everyone, finally, is alone. When the sky began to lighten, he walked once again to the pilot's casita in the village and found him building a small fire in his wood stove, a battered pan of milk and broken chocolate at the ready. "Ciudad de México, Ángel.

Ahora." He shoved the man out of his own house while pressing a jumble of pesos into his hand.

Chris rode shotgun in the little plane, one hand holding a cold *cerveza* and the other clutching the dashboard in front of him as Ángel banked quickly away from the coastline and headed north. Although flying all the way to Mexico City took longer than to Oaxaca, it would save him hours of time lingering in the Oaxaca airport, and Ángel hadn't complained, nor had he made mention of the disruption his regular flight schedule would suffer. They spoke little.

Chris gave the man—a father of five sons, two killed in car crashes on dark mountain roads, a third blinded in one eye by a firecracker—only the vaguest of details. Ángel nodded, gently made the sign of the cross, and kept his thoughts to himself for the duration of the flight. It wasn't until Chris was in Mexico City navigating his way around a maze of construction throughout the airport that he realized he had no luggage and was wearing only sandals, a pair of woven Guatemalan shorts, and a faded chambray shirt. How he had even remembered to bring his wallet— and his passport—was a mystery. Where the bills he had given Ángel had come from, he had no idea. A credit card got him his tickets from Mexico City to Houston and on to Albuquerque, and while he waited for the flight, he headed to a *casa de cambio* for some cash. He slid Nico's phony credit card in and out of the sleeve of his wallet several times. He had trouble swallowing.

He found a public phone and tried calling Melanie several times; it rang endlessly. Hopefully Camelia had made it to Melanie's side; she was the kind of friend who would try to do whatever it took, even if she didn't understand the circumstances. Hadn't she flown all the way to Dos Palmas on the flimsiest of stories from

Melanie? Christ, what a goat rodeo that had been; even he didn't exactly understand what that was all about. He wondered if he should try to contact Rayne.

He stood at a comically Old West-themed airport bar and ordered two shots of tequila, drank them quickly, and waited until the line of travelers heading onto the flight to Houston had dwindled to a final handful before forcing himself to join them. Being in the air over Dos Palmas had seemed like a dream, like the phone call he got last night —a sobbing, screaming Melanie, the calm voice of a police officer—hadn't even happened. But this—this getting on an Aeroméxico jetliner, suddenly forced into close quarters with a couple hundred strangers, climbing into a tin can that would hurl him through the sky toward Santa Fe and an unnameable pain—was something Chris did not think he could do.

Only the insistent *clack-clack* of the flight attendant's high heels behind him kept him moving toward the door of the plane.

Only the scent of her cheap perfume—and the glimpse of her cleavage in a too-tight uniform as he tried to turn around at the door and was pushed back into the plane by her very closeness and ripeness and a feeling that his stomach was turning inside out at the thought of this woman, any woman, so close to him at that moment or perhaps ever—kept him moving forward, stumbling toward his seat in a row blessedly unoccupied. He slouched in the window seat with his head against the glass, his legs stretched across the row, and closed his eyes.

Navigating the Houston airport, Chris bought some sweats and a pair of Nikes, washed his face in the men's room, and drank a margarita in a bar with real-time stock market quotes dizzily circling its perimeter. He went back to the men's room and threw up, washed his face again.

He bought a frozen yogurt just before getting on the plane. It was not quite two o'clock; for everyone else, it was any other afternoon on any other day. He would be in Albuquerque by four, in Santa Fe by five, six at the latest. He wondered what Melanie was doing.

And now in the cab heading home at last, the familiar landscape out the window, Chris finally tried to conjure up even a vague picture of Nico. He remembered the day the child was born, remembered holding him like a piece of blown glass, like lace made of tiny strands of candied sugar, like a handful of ball bearings that threatened to slip out of his fingers. He remembered him as a boy, five perhaps, running on the beach away from the waves, taunting them to come and get him, sneaking up on the crashing breakers, then running madly away again. One time the breaker caught him and threw him on the sand, and the undertow sucked him out into the water. Chris ran in after him and scooped him out, deposited him, laughing, on the dry sand yards from the water line. His hands on his knees, Chris had tried to draw a breath from lungs gone suddenly bone dry.

Snippets of memories darted in and out, scurrying away like a nocturnal beetle in a sudden glare of light. Melanie sitting in a weathered rocker with the two little kids toddling about at her feet on the portal of their beach house, a book on her lap forgotten as she kept track of the children's endless movements. Nico and Rayne helping each other learn how to surf, fishing with the village kids in the bay. Nico lingering on the beach for longer periods of time as more young people started to show up in Dos Palmas. Rayne crying behind the house one day because Nico had gone off with a cluster of teens from *los Estados Unidos* and left her behind. Nico at fifteen, one night on the beach, screwing that college girl, who should have known better anyway and who showed up at the hotel all moony eyed looking for him the next day, only to find herself talking to the boy's mother, of all people.

The cab pulled off the highway and began snaking its way downtown through the thickening traffic. Even Santa Fe had a rush hour now, Chris was surprised to note. He was disoriented by a row of chic apartment buildings in what had been an empty field on his last trip home. His stomach muscles, knotted for hours, ached; his breathing was shallow.

One thought had been hovering around the edges of his consciousness since the moment he'd gotten the phone call from the Santa Fe police last night. One dark, swollen thought that he continually pushed away whenever it came close enough for him to feel it sink into his brain and his heart and his tortured gut. One bleak, devastating feeling that he knew if he were to put a name to would cause him to sink into the ground like a house on a fault line, would snap his legs at the knees, would send his already fragmented life spewing into the cosmos like a hail of space garbage.

Relief.

He hated himself even as he acknowledged that finally, what he felt knowing all the wreckage would be cleaned up and they all would eventually go on with their lives, was relief. Relief that Nico's problems were over, relief that his and Melanie's problems with him were over, relief that now, as horrible as it sounded to himself, he had one less complication in his life. And he knew he would never dare admit out loud to anyone—and in fact, was thinking he could never even again admit to himself—that for at least one moment, he was relieved to hear his son was dead.

Yes, yes, he did hate himself now, and he knew he would forever on.

He directed the cabdriver to his street and then sat in the back seat for a moment, gazing at the house. The afternoon sky that had been bright when he landed in Albuquerque was now gray and threatening. Smoke rose from the chimney. The front curtains were drawn. An old Jeep Wagoneer was in the driveway; it had a Visualize Whirled Peas bumper sticker peeling off one corner. Probably Camelia's. And in front of it was Eric's pickup.

What the hell was Eric's pickup doing up here?

17 How Could He Have Forgotten the Wind?

Head bowed, eyes watering, and shoulders hunched against the chill, Eric hurried down the Paseo toward Marcy Street and the *Santa Fe Daily* office. It was close to eight, and traffic downtown was light. He had grabbed a knit cap and a wool scarf from the coatrack in Melanie's doorway—Nico's, probably—but they did little to mitigate the piercing effects of the wind. He wished he had snagged a warmer coat as well.

One thing he knew about February in Santa Fe: the weather changed almost constantly. When the peace of a sunny afternoon was suddenly broken by a dangerous hailstorm, when the sky put on a nonstop show of every sort of cloud imaginable, all layered one on top of the other in different shades of gray and purple, and yet a tiny patch of cerulean was still visible in between—ah, yes, spring was on its way.

How could he have forgotten the wind? He pulled open the front door of the newspaper office, grabbed a copy of the paper from a stack on the unattended front desk, and marched into the newsroom. He had no idea what he would say. He was as far out of his element as he could be.

Most of the desks were empty, and only a few people milled around near the coffee machine in a corner.

"Ulibarri? Federico Ulibarri?" Eric called out. In a doorway with Managing Editor on a sign overhead, two men stood deep in conversation. A tall, thin man with a graying mustache and rumpled denim shirt looked up quickly at the sound of Eric's voice. The other, in a white shirt with cuffs rolled up, tugged at his tie as though he'd like to rip it off and walk away. Eric shot a look directly at them and headed their way.

"We need to talk. *Now*." He held the paper in his fist, wishing it were a tire iron.

"Ah, you must be here about the shooting," the editor said, still fingering the knot in his tie. Ulibarri hovered close by.

"Please. Come right in," the man continued, his voice gaining authority. "Can I get you some coffee? I realize it seems like we have some kind of a problem here. And believe me, I am so sorry for your loss."

A keen new energy had begun to grow inside Eric. What did this guy know about his loss? If the last three years had been a sort of coma for him, he now felt fully alive and complete. He could feel his brain cells, once sodden with alcohol, sluggish and impotent, now firing off an internal chemistry he had forgotten existed. His confusion vanished.

"Don't schmooze me, pal," he said, electing to stay put in the newsroom instead of moving into the smaller office. "You bet we've got a problem. You know anything about this so-called rally on the Plaza this morning? You know anything about why this murdered teenager was misidentified on the front page today?" His voice was loud, his feet, rooted.

The reporters straggling into the newsroom halted in their tracks; the few people at the coffee machine looked up. Phones ringing on the desks went unanswered.

"Yes, yes, I understand you're upset, sir. I think we can figure out a way to fix this if we just take a moment to—"

"Fine, let's just make this quick. I have an appointment with the mayor." Eric started to follow both men into the small office. Three men in suits—not always a common sight in Santa Fe, he recalled, but one that usually indicated who was in charge—suddenly appeared, purposefully heading across the newsroom toward him.

"Oh, good, everybody's here, so I only have to say this once." Eric heard the sound of his voice and felt as though he were on a speeding train. Wait, he could hear inside of him, wait until you know what's going on. But what he knew was that the train was out of control, and he knew the track headed downhill, and he had no way of slowing down, no way of putting on the brakes, knew he was heading for a crash as surely as the words continued to tumble out of his mouth.

"Listen up, people. Nico Sullivan, your 'unnamed Hispanic teen,' is Anglo. He's not Hispanic. The cops knew that, too; they went to his house and took his mother to the morgue, so I don't know how you guys missed that annoying little detail. But my question is this: *Why should that even matter?* I don't know if Nico and his homies were breaking into that house or just hanging around too close to it. But how *dare* you turn this private tragedy into a racial episode?" His eyes fixed first on one person, then another, until he had made steely eye contact with everyone in the room.

"You guys better figure out how to fix this and do it now. The last thing the Sullivan family needs in their time of grief is a bunch of ignorant bigots spouting off. If there's any more bloodshed over this mess, you can bet it's going to be on your hands. Helluva lawsuit, don't you think?"

The men in suits hurriedly conferred with each other and quickly left the way they had come in, while the reporters stood calmly, their faces masks of passivity. He couldn't be sure they weren't mentally writing him off as a nutcase. One by one, they turned to their desks, dismissing him.

"Excuse me, sir—could you please identify yourself?" a young man called out to Eric, scribbling madly in his notebook.

Eric was exhausted. How could he get out of here? He walked up to the reporter, his voice suddenly dropping several decibels.

"What are you, twenty-two? Been a reporter long? You're the only one in this stinking place who knows what his job is. My name is Eric Steadman, family friend. You need to know anything about this stupid mess, you talk to me. Don't you dare burden the Sullivans with any more of this bullshit."

He slapped the newspaper onto the desk and headed out of the room. No one came after him. His hand was shaking as he pulled his cigarettes out of his jacket pocket on his way out the front door of the building. Once out on the street, he took a deep breath and felt as though he might collapse right there; he wondered if anyone would notice. Instead, he lit a smoke and started walking. If he remembered correctly, City Hall was just a few blocks away.

For the few moments he had been inside the newspaper office, Eric had successfully directed his thoughts away from the grief-filled Sullivan house, but now the enormity of the tragedy washed over him like an endlessly returning glacial tide. Loss. It bound them all together; Camelia as well had had her share. As for him? Perhaps too many losses to count, and most at his own hand, but now he knew he had also forever lost the seductive separation from his very self that he had cultivated the last few years. Sobriety and a cold February wind made sure he would never float on the surface of his own life again, no matter how he might long to.

Sprinting up the front walk of City Hall, he pulled on the locked front doors, peering through the glass and knocking. Someone had to be inside, Saturday or not. The mayor had stuck his foot in it last night talking to a reporter, and his comments were all over the city by now. Even while Eric had limited his own small world to one in which making smoothies and slicing oranges was enough, he had learned a thing or two listening to Chris talk about his dreams for the quiet beachfront village. It doesn't matter how smart your strategy might sound to you; you don't get to pick who monkey wrenches it. He kicked the metal plate at the bottom of the door.

The streets around him were quiet. He hoped the whole thing would blow over on its own, but he knew better. As if it were yesterday, that moment years before suddenly popped into his head, the trigger for his epic disappearing act, when a Santa Fe gardener made a sinister joke after helping him install some custom doors. "They think it's their town," the man had said, his fingers playing with a cigarette lighter. Eric could still hear his laughter.

He wrapped Nico's scarf a little more snugly around his neck and parked himself on a bench to figure out what to do next. He had about an hour until the rally, unless by some miracle the reporters at the *Daily* found a way to cut it off. New Mexico had its share of miracles; it would certainly take one for this mess to get cleared up.

The wind whipped around him. What was he doing here, anyway? Just a few moments ago he had been slicing oranges on the beach, he had been napping in his hammock. All of a sudden he was sitting outside, freezing, in Santa Fe, a teenager dead, his friends shattered, desire for one woman now constantly burning in his heart when he couldn't even remember the last time he had been with a woman nor had wanted to be, and somehow he was supposed to single-handedly prevent a riot on the Plaza.

Ayii, he was definitely the *gringo loco*. He watched a few well-dressed people hurrying by along Marcy Street. They held scarves to noses and pulled hats down over ears, tightened coat belts and shoved hands deeper into pockets. Tomorrow, they could all be in shirtsleeves. At least the sun was shining; the sky was clear and bright and not at all an indicator of the atmospheric violence on ground level.

As he sat there, a trio of women in well-worn winter jackets met at the corner from different directions and talked among themselves, stamping their feet against the cold but not appearing to be in any rush to move on. Three men across the street also came together, their jeans faded, their heavy plaid shirt jackets worn at the elbows. Another cluster gathered at the doorway of an old building down the block. Their solid, stained work boots toed the dry ground; they rubbed their rough hands together and blew on them for warmth.

Two chic blonde women in expensive-looking cowboy boots and long coats with colorful Native American blanket designs hurried past him, their faces steeled against the wind, their eyes straight ahead. After a moment or two of waiting to get through the small crowd on the corner, they finally separated and went around them, crossed the street, and hurried together into the real-estate office on the corner. They glanced back, their eyes slitted against the wind, only for a moment.

Eric sat up, digging his hands into his pockets. A man in a business suit tried to get into the building across the street but was blocked by a small but tightly packed group. They moved as a unit every time he tried to go around them until he gave up, crossed the street and hurried toward City Hall instead. "Did you see that?" he mumbled to Eric as he passed. "Fucking unbelievable."

A police car pulled up along Lincoln and turned onto Marcy, stopping for a moment directly in front of Eric. He watched as the various groups of people slowly spread out, ever so slightly creating the appearance of a bustling but moving crowd. The cop sat in his car; the people milled around, apparently unconcerned. Eric got up and walked purposefully away, heading down Lincoln toward the Plaza. In the doorways of Eddie Bauer and J. Crew and the Gap—stores he remembered newcomers and locals alike bitterly fighting against in Santa Fe's historic downtown—more little groups of people stood huddled together.

"Go home!" he heard shouted more than once, although it wasn't clear to Eric who was being yelled at. There were few tourists around on a blustery weekend, and all he saw were Santa Feans going to work at the local stores and galleries and nearby offices. His neck prickled with perspiration under Nico's scarf; his heart seemed to be beating outside of his jacket. The police car cruised by.

On the Plaza, Eric saw the city's maintenance workers struggling with rickety scaffolding for a temporary stage. Perhaps he could position himself behind it, stop the mayor before he got started. A television news van pulled up on Washington, but nobody got out. Suddenly, desperately, Eric wanted a drink.

And then he was falling to the ground, could see the sidewalk rise up to meet his arms, which he'd flung out awkwardly in hopes of recapturing his balance. He felt the cold concrete against his wind-burned cheek, something smashing up against his nose as all the softest parts of him were exposed in one long and dreadful moment. The sounds of running footsteps, loud young laughter, a police siren or maybe just the wind filled his ears.

"Whoa, shit, buddy, you okay? *¡Hijole!* What a mess; here's a handkerchief for that nose. Christ, I hope it's not broken." A man held his arm as he sat up on the cold sidewalk. Eric heard his chatter from far away; he thought he might vomit if he tried to stand. "Hey, you want to go inside someplace and clean up or something? Can you stand up?" No one else came near him.

"Tomás Rodríguez; I work at La Fonda. Just saw you go down, man. Here, let's try to get you standing up. You need 9-1-1? Where the hell's a cop when you need one? Seems like there's a few around here, but not for you and your broken nose, huh? Christ, just last night, you see the paper, bro? Poor kid gets shot, don't know why that guy didn't call the cops instead. Maybe he did and they didn't come. There, look, see, you're on your feet now, you want me to take you inside, make a call or something? You got people?"

Eric stared at the man. He was young, still perhaps in his twenties, and wore a white shirt under his denim jacket. His jeans were neat, his boots polished. He seemed impervious to the cold.

"No, thanks, gracias, man. I really appreciate the help. Don't know what just happened there. I think I'll be fine; really, thanks." Every muscle ached, his nose felt wet and soft. He gingerly brushed some grit from his arm and tested his elbow; his ragged appearance did not escape him.

"Look, man, you got someplace to go? You need some cash maybe?" Tomás reached into his back pocket for his wallet, but Eric stopped him.

"Seriously, I'm OK. Just got into town last night, haven't had time to change clothes or anything. Muchas gracias, Tomás."

"OK then. I need to get to work. They don't like it if you're late, even on a Saturday morning when the place is dead." He looked around, one hand still on Eric's shoulder. "Something going on here on the Plaza? I don't remember anything on the calendar. It's fucking February, man."

"I heard the mayor might be speaking today about, I don't know, something that maybe had to do with that kid getting shot," Eric said carefully, his eyes taking in the small knots of people bundled up in winter gear under the huge old cottonwoods, bare and the color of smoke. His original plan now seemed impossible.

"The mayor? That gasbag? I couldn't believe the bullshit he was spouting in the paper this morning." Tomás turned his head and spat at the curb.

Eric spotted a few reporters from the newspaper office on the other end of the Plaza. They were talking and laughing, casually scribbling in their notebooks. Through a gauze of pain, Eric watched as a large black raven directly above him circled the Plaza three times.

Someone climbed on the stage and began talking. He heard twenty or thirty men and women yelling back. And then, in the next moment, their voices floated away into the roar of rushing water. Their movements, hurried and sharp, now slowed to a fluid dance. Eric saw the ordinariness of the locals, Hispanic truck drivers and office workers, teachers and bank tellers and homemakers. And he saw helplessness and dismay. It was so like what he had seen in Dos Palmas—that is, on the few occasions he had allowed himself to be sober enough to look closely at Esperanza and her family and her neighbors—that he wondered if for a moment he were not hearing the rhythmic crashing of waves on the beach.

Tomás tried to steer him across the Plaza toward the La Fonda, but he was overcome with a sluggishness that made every movement a concerted effort. Perhaps he was actually underwater; maybe everyone else was.

Just as they made it to the hotel, several youths in oversized clothes and slicked-back hair appeared on San Francisco Street. The boys' fingers flashed signals in the air, their faces determined. The sudden sound of breaking glass up the street echoed like a bomb.

"Shit, get in here, man." Tomás pulled open the hotel doors and pushed Eric inside, where several of Tomás's colleagues were rushing through the lobby and shouting. Police sirens started up as more shop windows shattered across the sidewalks and the crowd broke, surging in every direction.

It was Melanie who first pulled the bottle from a kitchen cabinet shortly after Eric walked in the door, bloodied and swaying. Ah, yes: *la medicina*. He waved it away even as his mouth began to water and asked her for some ibuprofen instead. Melanie, after a few sips, checked out his injuries with unexpected focus. Camelia hovered nearby, taking a quick swallow from the bottle herself and following Melanie's instructions for finding the first aid kit in the bathroom cabinet.

Melanie did not let Eric say a word about what had happened to him downtown. She demanded silence from both of them during her ministrations and then abruptly walked back into the living room and burrowed into her cave of blankets, leaving them both at the kitchen table. Camelia's eyes were ringed red and swollen.

"I suppose I could use a glass, pretend this is just a normal day and I'm having a normal drink, even though I don't normally drink this early in the day unless I'm on vacation, but you already know that," Camelia said. She sat across from him, her fingers absently chipping at the grooves in the tabletop, the bottle in front of her. "Are you sure you won't join me? I seem to recall you have quite a taste for it."

His ears still rang, and he couldn't quite sort out exactly how he had gotten hurt, what had happened. There were ravens, he remembered that. He was swimming. There was Tomás. There were Esperanza and Miguel, making bread in the firelight.

"Look, she's asleep again, you can talk to me now, Eric." She took his hands gently in hers and kissed the purpling skin. He sighed; he felt his throat constrict.

"You know, last night, when I was driving up here, I began to feel a kind of, I don't know, calm about being back here," he began. "I hadn't given Santa Fe a thought for years, but suddenly, I was getting all sort of, you know, really kind of stoked about it. I saw this bumper sticker on the car in front of me as I came into town: *Creemos en los Sueños*. Where else can you go where even the bumper stickers tell you to believe in your dreams?" He laughed a little, until it turned into a cough. Camelia grabbed a coffee cup from the sink, rinsed it out, and filled it with water for him.

"I remembered when I first came here, how it seemed to sort of... heal me," he went on. "Yes, that's right. Heal. My life had been a mess for so long, and when I left New York, I barely got out alive. After I found this place, it seemed like for once, I could just put my head down and sleep."

He winced at a small spasm somewhere in his rib cage.

"It was small, and it was quiet, and the air was so clear, and the people seemed so real. I lived in the barrio, right off Agua Fria, and I hung out with my neighbors. I had holidays with them, they took me in like I was one of their own. Most of them Hispanic, locals, you know? They didn't care that I wasn't from here. Nobody did. Seems like people have been coming here from other places forever; why is it suddenly such a big deal to some people? I spent time up north learning the wood carving and felt like I really belonged here. Hell, I learned how to fix the crumbling adobe on my casita, even though I was just renting it."

He stopped, he drank more water, he couldn't bring his eyes to meet Camelia's.

"And when Shelley got pregnant and moved in with me and we got married, at first, I really felt like I had made it to some kind of finish line, I had survived my life and my youth and now I was a real person, it was official. I made a child. And so I caulked the windows and glazed the brick floors, and I actually started carving a fucking cradle."

Eric wiped his eyes. Only the gentle pressure of Camelia's warm hand on his cheek, the scent of her hair as she leaned close to him, brought him back to the surface.

"I loved that kid. I did," he whispered to her. "That was a right shitty thing I did, leaving them. What kind of an asshole would do that?"

Camelia wrapped her arms gently around his aching shoulders, placed the tenderest kiss on his neck, and rested her head against his heartbeat. The pain pushed aside for now, he stood, pulling her up with him, and kissed her fully and deeply. The mezcal on her tongue was like nectar; he held her so tightly every surface of their bodies seemed without boundary. And he pushed the collar of her sweater back as he placed his lips on her neck and tasted her skin, and for an eternal moment he wanted to engulf her, to embody her, to take her inside of him as surely as he wanted now to be inside of her.

Her eyes were filled with tears, and he kissed their edges, tasted the salt, and held her close. His confusion this morning on the Plaza had vanished. The grief in Melanie's house was forgotten. Now he knew only one thing.

"Stay with me, Camelia. Stay with me," he said, his face buried in her hair, his lips grazing her ear.

Eric sat in the kitchen alone, the little television on with the sound muted. After hours of difficult conversation, many tears, and some awkward dozing at the table, Camelia had gone upstairs to take a shower. Melanie, who had gotten slightly drunk earlier in the day, still slept on the couch in the living room. The clear bottle with no label sat on the table, three inches of pale mezcal releasing its musky aroma to the room.

Now and then he glanced at the screen, spattered with drops of food and grease and a layer of dust, and waited for the first newscast of the afternoon. He munched a piece of toast with peanut butter on it. He thought of Camelia upstairs in the shower, warm water and fragrant soap sliding across her slippery body; he wanted to be in there with her. He wondered whether she had seen her husband since she returned.

She had cracked him open, sitting there across from him this morning, sitting there with him after he had fallen and swum and flew. He imagined waking up tomorrow morning next to her, this nightmare of the Sullivans behind them.

The wind picked up, and the back door began to rattle; the sky had taken on a leaden sheen. He turned the volume up slightly as the opening credits for the news came on. The front door handle clicked twice and then jiggled against the lock. Eric hurried to the window and slid open the edge of the curtain. Chris, incongruous in a fresh sweat suit and white trainers, a day's worth of stubble on his cheeks, sagged on the portal as though he might collapse. Thick snow flurries blew in the air. Eric opened the door against the biting wind, a finger to his lips as he pointed to Melanie crashed out on the couch, and hurried Chris into the kitchen.

". . . an apparent misunderstanding over the identity of a young burglar allegedly killed by the owner of the house he was breaking into led to this morning's mayhem on Santa Fe's Plaza," the anchorman was saying. "While originally reported to be Hispanic, the dead youth was apparently an Anglo, although that information did not reach the mayor's office in time to stop the rally . . ."

"What? What the hell is he talking about?" Chris stood transfixed in front of the television.

"We go now to Kristina Meyers, on the Plaza live, where city crews are cleaning up the debris from the window-breaking spree this morning. Kristina? Quite a scene up there, wouldn't you say?" The anchorman's unctuous manner, his perfectly blow-dried hair and carefully knotted tie, brought sudden bile to Eric's throat.

"That's right, Tom, things are a mess here on the Plaza. Windows are broken, park benches torn up, some cars on the perimeter have been damaged. While it doesn't appear there was any looting this afternoon, the destruction of property is already being estimated in the tens of thousands of dollars." She stood at a corner of the Plaza, her dark coat pulled tightly around her, red lipstick glaring.

Chris did not move, not through the blaming of a local gang for the damage, not through the interviews with various city officials on the Plaza this morning, not through the almost-in-passing clarifications of Nico's identity.

When the reporter wrapped up the story with an excited teaser about bad weather on its way and the first advert came on, Eric reached over and switched the TV off. He pulled out a chair and steered Chris into it, putting the bottle of mezcal in front of him. Camelia, her damp hair curling softly around her face, appeared in the doorway of the kitchen. No one spoke for several minutes.

And then a small pillow came sailing through the doorway, barely missing Camelia but hitting Chris squarely on the shoulder. Another pillow flew in, this one knocking the mezcal bottle over, followed by a barrage of pillows, shoes, and finally the small clay bowl Eric had been using as an ashtray. Next came Melanie, her pitching arm still heaving items at close range. She fell upon Chris and began pummeling him, crying, screaming. And then her flailing arms came to rest on his chest, and she slid down to her knees and exhaled great, wrenching sobs and moans and buried her face in his knees.

It was more life than Melanie had shown to Eric and Camelia since they'd arrived, and they quickly stepped out of the kitchen. Eric looked back once. Chris had put his hands gently on Melanie's hair and doubled over to cradle her, then pushed himself off the chair and onto the floor, still holding the wailing Melanie, and they stayed there long after the day's light had faded from the windows.

18 It Simply Is This Way

"Hey, you guys better get a move on, it looks like a fucking blizzard out there," Chris called up to Camelia and Eric from the bottom of the stairs. Camelia was so stiff from sitting, straightening up was almost painful; they had been huddled on the top step of the narrow stairway for hours. Earlier they had debated whether they should sneak back down the stairs and try to quietly leave. Would they perhaps announce their departure? Or instead, should they stick around and offer to, what, cook dinner, order something in, make phone calls? She couldn't stand the sound of her friends' hearts breaking apart; she couldn't bear to stay in that house another minute. Finally she had rested her head on Eric's shoulder. "The hell with it," she had said, "let's just wait until they tell us what to do," and promptly dozed off. Now Eric nudged her gently.

"Thank God," she whispered. "How's your truck in the snow? Do you want to leave it here or follow me?"

"I will follow you. I will always follow you." His voice rasped, his lips brushed her ear. She shivered.

In the living room, the fire was reduced to embers. Melanie sat on the couch dry-eyed, emanating an aura of clarity of purpose so strong Camelia looked around, wondering at first what had changed. It almost seemed as though Melanie had rearranged the furniture, so different was the feeling in the room. Chris stood at the window and peered into the night. No one spoke. Camelia pulled her coat on, with no idea what time it was, how much snow there might be outside, what she should say.

Eric put his hand on Chris's shoulder, but Chris let it rest for only a moment before shrugging it off. "Get going, *hermano*," he said, his voice rough. "Thanks for everything and all that. I'll take it from here. We'll be in touch." He never turned from the window. Camelia bent to hug Melanie, who looked away and began picking at the edge of a blanket. Grief cannot be explained, Camelia knew. It tears you apart, fills your gut with broken glass. When you try to wrap logic around it and find you can get nowhere at all, it squeezes your mind into a tiny ball. She took Eric's hand and let him lead her out the front door.

Snow swirled about them in the darkness. The cold air slapped her cheeks. They stood on the portal in silence until hoarse voices rose from inside the house.

She loved the solitude of living out in the country, Camelia had told him that afternoon, and rarely felt vulnerable except when the weather was bad and the driving became treacherous. Once, while driving home, a sudden summer hailstorm began pounding her car like the bullets of an assault weapon. Rattled by the barrage of ice, she had stopped the car in the middle of the road and screamed until the storm blew over a few minutes later. Now, as she picked her way through the snow to her car, she reiterated her vow to move into town as soon as it was even remotely possible.

Driving slowly through the darkness with Eric half a block behind her, she kept his one good headlight—slightly askew—visible in her rearview mirror, even during the long and grueling trip back down Cerrillos Road, where cars slid and spun around them. Drivers trying to get home quickly to beat the worst of the storm made the road a nightmarish game of luck. At times, the heavy snowfall reduced visibility to a few yards at best, and once the traffic lights got stuck on blinking yellow, all sense of order vanished.

Not daring to go more than twenty the entire trip, she let herself breathe fully when she finally turned off the major thoroughfare an hour after starting out. With the bright lights of the city behind her, she struggled to find her way on dark rural roads thick with snow. The occasional crooked reflector poking out of the drifts kept her from driving into the ditch. Sheer instinct alone led her to her own driveway and her little house, hunkered in darkness. She was sure the porch light had been on when she'd left last night. A quick glance around her confirmed her dread.

Eric stood behind her on the front portal, his arms wrapped gingerly around her while she struggled with her key at the darkened door. Once in, Camelia flipped the light switch several times. "Oh, great. Shit."

The moment of nervous anticipation she felt with his warm breath on the back of her neck evaporated as she made her way to the kitchen cabinets and pulled out a large glass Our Lady of Guadalupe votive candle. From the doorway, Eric held his lighter out as a beacon; their faces took on a shadowy glow. The house was cold.

"Where's the firewood? I'll bring some in." He stamped the snow off his shoes on the front portal.

"Just to the side there. Better bring in a lot."

The wind had become ferocious. They struggled with the firewood, dumping an extra armload near the front door, where she hoped it would stay dry. Camelia was grateful for her nest of blankets on the floor in front of the fireplace; it was obvious that would be the warmest place in the house. She located more candles and placed them on the windowsills in silence while Eric got the fire going.

"I can't believe how dark it is out there," she said finally, her eyes flickering past his beat-up old sneakers next to the front door, neatly set like they belonged there. The noise of the storm buffeted the tiny house. It made her feel queerly dislocated, as though she could be anywhere or was perhaps instead nowhere, and she could be anyone, anyone at all. No longer the same Camelia Delmonico staring out the window of the house where she had tried to figure out who she was until the day she met Michael and decided it was time to marry.

No longer the Camelia who had endured far longer than she should have the limbo of a relationship gone sour and a job that did nothing but kill time.

Not even the Camelia who had left Santa Fe on a gray February dawn to find herself embraced in warm salt air and the arms of a stranger, not to mention thoroughly entangled in a complex family drama she didn't fully understand.

The fire sputtered. She wanted the flames to reach out and weave around her, to let her new self—whoever that might be—rise Phoenix-like from the ashes, clear and pink and unblemished.

"Talk about being stranded on a desert isle," Eric said, squatting in front of the fireplace and leaning back on his heels to look at her standing at the window, firelit. Camelia was silent. Her breathing felt short and shallow; she wondered if she might swoon. Her legs went unsteady with desire, and she leaned back on the windowsill for a moment to get her bearings.

"Take your coat off, Camelia, it's warm in here now," he said, his voice a whisper. The firelight filled the room with an amber glow and the beguiling scent of piñon; the candles added the musk of sandalwood, their lights shimmering like stars against the window.

He took her hands and led her down to the pile of blankets in front of the fireplace. She was made of liquid. She felt his lips tentatively brush across hers and dance slowly down her neck and across her throat, she felt his hands on her skin. She could scarcely breathe; she could explode at any minute. She would cascade out into the universe in a million sprinkles of glassy light; she would rain sparkles onto the dark, snow-covered land.

She felt worshipped, underneath him in a pool of fire. She rocked and she moaned; she pulled him to her tightly; she rose to meet him and slipped back, rose and slipped back; she sighed deeply into his ear; and, as though she were inside the warm, soft wax of the candles, she felt herself merge into light as he pulsed inside her and released a shower of stars.

While snow danced and blew outside the windows, the candles became solid puddles on the windowsills, fingers of wax reaching down the wall below. She couldn't sleep; too many stories crowded inside her. She knew the disturbance on the Plaza would be forever forgotten in the aftermath of the blizzard. Nico's death would become unremarkable in the face of storm-related fatalities. Chris and Melanie either would never bother to call Rayne in Ireland and kill each other in their living room, or would reconcile so beautifully that from now on they would think of Nico's death only as the blessing it was surely disguised to be.

The wind roared across the frozen landscape and pushed at the little house, rattling the windows and whooshing in the chimney. She looked at Eric, dozing; for a moment, she had no idea who he was or what he was doing here, tangled up within her blankets, his leg entwined with hers.

He stretched against her and reached his arm across to pull her closer. He smiled, burying his face in her hair. Earlier he had said, "Stay with me." She hadn't answered then and still had no idea as to how she would answer if he asked again. "Stay with me"—what did that mean? Never leave my side, make a life with me, make love with me always and forever? It had been so easy to consider that in the abstract with Michael, who had never brought starfire on his fingertips to mark her body, had never cupped her face in his hands nor spoken with urgency in her ear.

She had ignored what she knew she was doing with Michael, stuffed it down like one of those kid's toys, the snake made out of a spring that you shove into a can. She just put a lid on it, so clearly doomed from the beginning it was a wonder she was able to sleep at night, knowing all along the whole thing was going to blow up in her face.

At the thought of Michael, she vividly recalled her wedding day: sitting in the bathroom, her dress hanging on a hook on the door, legs heavy and stomach queasy. Her heart had pounded erratically and the moisture under her arms threatened to drip down her sides. Her forehead felt too tight for her face and her hair follicles prickled at her scalp like thousands of pinpoints. She had gripped the basin but refused to look at herself in the mirror; she considered sinking through a hole in the floor or climbing out the window or slitting her wrists, perhaps.

Now, as Eric woke and stroked her hair and began to talk earnestly about what they might plan together, Camelia felt herself pulling away. She didn't want to make plans, she didn't want to look at her feelings for him, she didn't want to listen to him. One thing had already been decided by Eric himself, years ago; she knew there would never be a baby with this man. A pair of tears slowly glided down her cheeks.

"Are you afraid of what I want?" he said after she was silent for a long while, the firelight and shadows obscuring his expression. "Or of what you want?"

"I don't know," she readily admitted. "I don't know how I feel, and I don't know what I want, and I don't want to know either of those things yet about you." The wind outside was loud in her ears. "No, you're right, I am afraid. I'm afraid that no matter what I say you'll be on the opposite end of the spectrum. Or else you won't be— maybe you're right there where I am, wherever that is— and maybe that's what I'm afraid of too. Because how do I know if that's going to be a good thing for me after everything, all the, I don't know, bad choices I made where I didn't really look at what I was doing?"

She felt as distant from him at this moment as she had that day they had walked back to the Paloma Blanca after drinking away the afternoon, when she'd exposed herself as a soggy, teary mess.

"Camelia, do you think you made bad choices?"

She stared at him.

"Do you? I mean, what did you do that a million, a billion other people haven't also done? Did you fall in love with the wrong person?" He raised his hand like a schoolboy. "Did you get married before you really understood what it meant, before you were really prepared, maybe for the wrong reasons? Here again. Did you fall out of love with your spouse? Hello, member of the club here. Are those really bad choices, sweetheart, or are they just part of the whole thing, just things that happen during life, steps along the way?"

Camelia was silent. Maybe it just meant they had both made bad choices, in which case they were either perfect for each other or disastrous.

"I used to think that, yeah, everybody makes mistakes, and I'm entitled to a few of my own," he said, poking at the fire and sending a shower of sparks cascading up the wind-filled flue.

"Then one night, when I was sitting on my portal listening to the waves and sipping from a little bottle of mezcal and feeling sorry for myself for what a lousy mess I had made of my life—my kid lost, no one to love, really just wasting away in a lonely, remote village on the edge of the planet—I began to wonder if maybe those things weren't mistakes at all, weren't bad choices or even stupid choices, but just . . . choices. Just the things I did that brought me to that place, there on the beach that night in a moment of quiet when I found myself facing who I was and what I had become." He didn't look at her.

"I wondered if maybe there really *wasn't* a right way and a wrong way to do certain things—things like the path your life takes or the way you have relationships—because if there wasn't, then there wouldn't be things like mistakes or bad choices. It simply is. It simply is this way. Who's to say that if I had done things differently, it might not have turned out exactly the same? Who's say if I had stayed with Shelley and sobered up and made some plans with her, I wouldn't have lost my boy? I still might have lost him some other way. Jesus, look at Chris and Melanie.

"And anyway, who's to say I might not still be sitting in the back room of that house with a bottle of vodka and my carving tools, and maybe one night I would decide to carve my own arm up just for a little change of pace? Who's to say that if I had never even come to New Mexico but stayed in New York, I might still not have somehow wound up in Dos Palmas running my little shake shack and wondering what the fuck I was doing with my life, until the day the most beautiful and lonely woman I'd ever seen walked in and shook up my secure, drunken little world like a fucking earthquake?"

The man on the plane, his Tarot cards spread out in front of him, flashed behind Camelia's eyes. "That sounds suspiciously like you are talking about fate."

"No, I don't mean it that way. I don't mean that no matter what you do you are still going to end up in the same certain place." Eric rolled onto his back with his palms beneath his head. "It's more like, not that certain outcomes are fated to happen no matter what you do, but more that no matter what you do, there's no way of knowing if things would have been different, or better, or somehow less wrong if you had done them a different way instead. Do you understand?"

"I'm not sure," she said finally. "If there aren't bad choices or good choices in a relationship, just different paths to choose, how is anyone ever supposed to know if they are doing the right thing?"

"Look, baby, stop flagellating yourself over a relationship gone bad." He rolled onto his side, his head propped on his palm, and looked at her. "Love isn't logical. Desire isn't rational. Passion isn't something you can cook up with a recipe. People come together for all kinds of reasons, but if you don't have that love, or desire, or passion, then maybe it's worth reconsidering.

"And things end," he went on, and Camelia heard echoes of Melanie that night at Casa Abuelita, when she'd hoped for a little sympathy over her missing husband and instead found herself with a plane ticket and a hangover. "Things end," Melanie had said of Camelia's marriage, redirecting the conversation to a discussion of her certainty that Nico had run away to be with his father in Mexico, needing only her help to prove it to be true. Now Camelia wondered if perhaps she had really been talking about her own life with Chris all along.

"People grow, and yes, they do grow apart," Eric said. "Or else they stand still while the world changes around them. Yeah, maybe you guys could have talked about things more and come to some kind of common decision, instead of him walking out, you blowing town, him trashing your place, you meeting someone else. God knows I could have done things differently too, but I didn't, and I can't change that. Look. Do you think you have something to atone for? Do you think you're supposed to suffer now or deny yourself a little pleasure, perhaps? Hmm?"

With that, his gaze softened, and he reached out a hand to stroke her cheek. Her confusion fled, and she came back to the one thing she had known since the moment she saw him: she wanted him, and the rest, all of it, didn't matter.

19 A Good Time for a Clean Start

Eric woke early Sunday morning to a sky the color of bone. He knew these mountain storms came on quickly and rarely lasted. It was no longer snowing, and it was entirely possible that the sun would be out later. Camelia slept. Oh, he was hardly the person to tell her everything was going to work out all right. Sure, he sounded like he knew what he was talking about last night. But in the bleached light of morning, he realized his philosophizing had just been his way of letting himself off the hook, and a damn big hook it was at that. He stood at the window for several minutes before he realized the pinpoints of light outside, barely glowing in the morning white, were porch lights. He looked around the room; the VCR clock blinked 00, as if signaling it was already the beginning of the end of this particular limbo. Panic flared in his chest.

How lovely she is, he thought as he watched her sleep. She was so real; she never hid from him. Her eyes could well up at a moment's notice; he could feel her heart breaking or see her joy like a beacon in the night. The way she always wanted to figure things out—hell, he had spent most of *his* life shutting himself down or running away. In the last week, she had opened every door inside him with little more than an honest kiss and the touch of her fingers on his arm. The very thought terrified him. But no, he was not going to walk away this time.

And then there was Zane. The boy wouldn't know him now; he probably didn't even remember the short time he had lived with his father and mother together. His son was what, close to two? when Eric found himself on the far edge of New Mexico and unable to make himself turn around. It had been three long years since then; a lifetime. He had told Camelia last night that he had no intention of tearing Zane away from his mother. "I just want to see him, tell him I'm here, I exist." She hadn't answered; he knew there was nothing she could say.

He ran his hands through his hair and wondered if the pipes were frozen. If not, maybe he should just grit his teeth and jump into a cold shower for a few minutes to clear his head. He abandoned the idea almost as soon as thought of it. Instead he wandered into the kitchen and found the furnace behind a door. He lit the pilot, and the machine chugged to life; moments later, warm air was blowing through the registers. Camelia didn't stir. Eric peeked into the two back rooms. Standing in the doorway of her bedroom, he felt unwilling to cross the threshold. Warm peach walls were trimmed with lavender baseboards and windowsills; a shopping bag with new sheets spilled onto the bare mattress. The closet door, slightly ajar, revealed a jumble of clothes, shoes, and hangers piled on the floor.

He remembered Camelia telling him about her languid inability to do much about the mess she discovered after her return. It made him think of Shelley and the day he didn't come home as expected. The thought made him ache all over. He turned away, glancing into the other room, which was completely empty save for a tattered telephone book on the floor, and headed back toward the living room.

A moment later Eric retraced his steps and retrieved the phone book. He sat at the kitchen table for several minutes, wishing for coffee, jonesing for a cigarette, his fingers drumming on the phone book, rubbing absently against the stubble of his cheeks. He looked at the purple cabinets, the pink refrigerator; it was like a dollhouse kitchen, sweet and lighthearted. He wanted to somehow stretch his arms all the way around the house and hug it close to him.

He thumbed the phone book. Finally, flipping it open, with the solid awareness it would be there, he found the name Shelley Steadman. The address and the phone number were the ones he had left behind; only his own existence was erased.

Oh, *Madre de Dios*; there was no turning back now. He glanced at Camelia, who had murmured and rolled over. Should he call or just show up, go alone or take Camelia with him? Walking into the heavily drifted snow until he dropped was the sort of thing he would have imagined as an option a few days ago, but now that seemed ridiculous. He had no idea what time it was, but he heard the slow grind of heavy machinery in the distance and realized the neighborhood was already being plowed. He couldn't even count on the blizzard to hide him.

Eric had no idea what he would say to Shelley if he called. He had no words to explain why he simply drove past their street one day and kept going and never went back. He couldn't say what he was feeling then, and he couldn't make any sense of it now. Shame welled up in him with the force of a fever. All that time he had spent quelling it with mezcal and pulque, he knew it was there. His self-loathing was a spiny monster coiled inside him that needed a steady dose of alcohol just to be kept at bay. How pathetic that he actually believed he could tame that beast. Without a drink for several days, it was slowly coming back to life, its once-besotted fangs now sharp and eager and ready to rip him apart from the inside out. He reached for the phone, determined to call Shelley and beg for forgiveness.

"Food, I need food," Camelia moaned, stretching herself awake underneath the blankets. "Must . . . have . . . green . . . chile . . ."

Eric hastily closed the phone book and said a silent thank-you as he stepped to the pile of blankets and tried to scoop them up, Camelia included, in his arms. "Hey, sleepyhead, time's a-wastin'. The lights are on, the furnace is cranking, the snowplow's out there this minute. We better get into town for some green chile before every *norteño* this side of the Rio Grande gets there first." Her laughter brought him back from the edge, pushing the beast back down into the darkness, even if only for a short while.

Camelia snapped the sheet pocket onto the corner of the mattress and flattened out the creases. Eric had left the bathroom door ajar while he showered; soft wisps of moisture infiltrated the stuffy house. She flung open the flat sheet like a parachute several times and let it drift lazily to the bed. The nagging internal questions that had plagued her about what she, and he, and they were going to do next no longer mattered. "It is what it is," she remembered him saying. *And it'll be whatever it's going to be.*

In a fit of activity, she reset all the clocks, cleaned up the melted wax from the windowsills, and gathered up the blankets and hung them on the line in the yard to air out.

They smelled of piñon smoke and sex, and she almost stopped herself from taking them outside at all. The closet would be next. The house would become hers again, piece by piece.

By noon the sun had come out with a vengeance, as though it had missed its daily routine and was busy trying to catch up, melting the deep snowdrifts. It sent flashes of brilliance everywhere. Camelia located her landlord's old snow shovel around the back of the house and handed it to Eric for the front walk while she swept the heavy, wet snow from their vehicles. A snowplow, painted bright red with curly white letters proclaiming We Cater Weddings! along the side, came by and cleared the driveway for them before going on its way, one gloved hand waving from the driver's window.

"Ready for breakfast?" he called to her. "That place Tortilla Flats still there?" He had finished scraping the rest of the snow from the walk, but the effort was merely a formality; the snow was melting so quickly it was hard to believe it had been well over a foot deep at dawn.

"Yeah, it's still the first place to eat you hit once you get into town from here. Works for me; I'm going through green chile withdrawal." Camelia ran inside for her keys and purse, locked the door behind her on her way out, and climbed into her Wagoneer, where Eric waited for her. Without the snow cover, the ground was rapidly turning to mud. She knew the road would be soup by the time they came back.

"Good thing the snow's clearing up so fast. There's a lot to do. First, though, I'm going to call Shelley." He gazed out his window. "Turns out she's still here, according to the phone book, anyway. So I think maybe I'll go over there later and check things out. See what's going on with her and Zane."

Camelia concentrated on the road ahead.

"Sounds like a good idea," she said after a moment. Her heartbeat had gone off track. "Maybe sort of tie up some loose ends?"

"Yeah, just see what they're doing, see if she'd let me see Zane, you know, regularly." His words hung in the stillness.

Traffic on Cerrillos Road was a little sparser than usual but just as erratic. Santa Feans have very short memories about some things, Camelia thought as she navigated carefully among the speeding cars to get to the restaurant entrance. They'd probably already forgotten the snow, even though rapidly melting piles of the stuff lined the busy street.

"So we are short staffed, and we have a limited menu," the waitress said as soon as they sat down. "But we did manage to get some supplies in around dawn, so, you know, we have plenty of eggs and chile and bacon and tortillas and cheese and coffee, of course. You know what you want, hon?"

Once they ordered, Eric went to get a paper from the row of boxes in front of the restaurant. They were mostly empty, he reported back to her; there was no paper from Albuquerque at all, and the *Santa Fe Daily* was just a single section with plenty of snow coverage and a promise to return to its normal printing schedule on Monday, once it could pull enough staff back into the office.

"And Nico? That rally on the Plaza?" She sipped her coffee, grateful for its bitter warmth.

"Nothing. Unbelievable. Maybe you're right; maybe it'll be completely forgotten," Eric said. He flipped through the pages again. "Maybe the best thing Melanie and Chris could do now is just get out of town. They don't need to be here. Too many bad memories." He tossed the paper onto a nearby chair.

"You know, I've been wondering if maybe leaving town might be a good thing for me, too." Camelia surprised herself with her words. She had been thinking no such thing at all, at least not since that day at Luis's house, when she'd scribbled a list of everything in Santa Fe she'd miss. By the first night at the Paloma Blanca with Nico and Eric, she had already talked herself out of thinking she could just stay there on the beach and forget about her life back in Santa Fe. And yet there it was, as though she had just laid a giant egg on the table. She saw a flash of naked panic on Eric's face before he regained himself. She wondered why she had even said such a thing.

"Really? For a trip or for good?"

"I don't know. I just started to think again about how tired I am of Santa Fe. Everything feels done, finished. You know that feeling? I was thinking about how I was going to have to look for a job, and make some kind of arrangements with Michael, probably just filing some kind of paperwork or something, but I'll probably have to see him, and it just made me feel very. . . tired. This is a small town, you know, not as small as Dos Palmas, but small just the same. This might be a good time for a clean start somewhere new."

Eric was silent, but he held her gaze until she looked away. She tore her napkin into tiny pieces, unable to look at him again. She felt herself sinking.

"Sounds to me like you're thinking of running away. Trust me, I recognize the signs." His voice held a harshness she had not heard before. "You probably don't want to hear this, but I'll say it anyway. You'll take all your shit with you, babe, and it'll hang around your neck like a rope with a rock on it. I'm not saying you have to stay put in one place, and if you're sick of this town, then by all means, leave. Just don't think you're leaving your problems behind. They go where you go, and they don't go away until you deal with them. You gotta give me credit for figuring something out these last few years on the beach."

"It just seems so overwhelming. I can't even bear the thought of facing him." A huge cloud of regret fell on her; she was so ashamed at how thoughtless she had been, how careless with Michael's heart, with her own.

"Oh, right, you think I'm looking forward to seeing Shelley? You don't have the market cornered, Camelia. Just get on with it. It'll be one less thing to worry about. Then you can think a lot more clearly about what you want to do with your life—including moving away, if that's what you think you need." He leaned back as the waitress placed the hot dishes in front of them.

Of course he was right; she didn't know what she was talking about. She had no intention of leaving town right now. She'd be crazy to think relocating would be any easier than what awaited her this week right here. It was just one more thing she found herself saying without thinking it through. Besides, she didn't even have any money, let alone any sort of plan, and she certainly didn't want to leave Eric. Her feelings for him were so strong, she was a little afraid of them; Camelia could admit that much.

Avoiding his eyes, she instead watched the waitress as she bustled back to the kitchen, almost bumping into a woman with a small child as they came out of the bathroom. She stared at the boy; he was lean and slight, perhaps five years old, and had a shock of golden hair that gleamed. He looked like a miniature version of Eric.

Camelia froze as she watched the woman and the boy walk toward them on their way to the front door. They would be passing right by her and Eric in a matter of seconds. Eric had just started eating when he saw the expression on her face and turned around to see what she was looking at. The woman turned back to pull the boy along with her, and when she looked ahead again, she saw Eric. Her hand flew to her mouth.

"Shelley. Jesus, Zane . . ." Shelley didn't move, but the boy began to tug on her hand. She scooped him up in her arms with a speed that astonished Camelia, hurried past them, and ran out the door.

Eric jumped out of his chair so quickly it fell over behind him and he almost tripped over the leg. "Shelley, wait!" After struggling to catch his balance, he ran after them.

Camelia stared at the plate in front of her, the heavy layer of melted cheese a gelatinous mass, the soupy green chile surrounding everything; her stomach constricted. She pulled a warm tortilla out of the basket, tore off a small piece, dipped it in the chile, and nibbled at it. She was starving, but she pushed the plate away. Finally she looked out the window, where she could see Eric in the parking lot, trying to talk to Shelley. He looked distraught; he might even be crying. Shelley held Zane tightly, awkwardly; her face was angry. She pointed at Eric several times with a stabbing motion and turned away from him. He went after her, and she turned again, and they yelled some more.

A busboy came by and righted Eric's chair, glancing out the window and lingering for a moment to watch the domestic unrest outside. Camelia made another half-hearted attempt at her breakfast and thought about how she would feel if she were in Shelley's position. She'd be pissed, that's what she'd be. Did he think Shelley was just going to say, "Welcome back, come on over and play with your son"? She stole another look out the window and felt her heart dive. The three of them were huddled together,

Eric's arms wrapped around Shelley and Zane. She could see the tears on Shelley's face, the boy hiding in his mother's arms, Eric wiping his eyes, ruffling the boy's hair. No one was smiling. He kissed Zane on the forehead, and Shelley and the boy turned away.

He came back inside and sat down, put his head in his hands, and was silent.

"Shall we go? I seem to have lost my appetite," she said after several minutes.

He looked at her, his eyes so sad Camelia thought she might die. She wanted to embrace him, but she couldn't make herself move. She wanted to be soft, but she felt hard; she was going to lose him after all. She needed a plan, fast. Seattle, too wet; San Francisco, too expensive; Phoenix, too hot.

"She said for me to come over tonight, that she wanted to think about everything but maybe there might be a way that I could see Zane once in a while as long as I wasn't thinking of taking him away. She's got a boyfriend; they're happy together." He wiped his eyes. "God, what a relief. I didn't realize how much I was dreading making that phone call, and now I don't have to. Wow. That was the last thing I would have expected."

Revived, he sent back his breakfast to be reheated. When the waitress returned with the hot plate, he attacked it.

"Maybe Michael will show up too," Camelia said. "Maybe rear-end my car while I'm pulling out of the parking lot or something." She shredded her cold tortilla, still unable to eat.

"Man. I just can't believe that. In a million years, I wouldn't have expected to just run into her—into them— like that. Shit. I thought I would just crash right through the sidewalk when she started screaming at me for being such a fuckup. But you know what? I didn't. I was actually relieved to get it over with so fast. God, what a beautiful kid. I can't believe him, he's just … I can't get over it. I barely had this vague image of him in my mind when he was a tiny thing, and look at him, he's like five or something. Amazing. I wonder if he goes to school or what, if he draws or plays ball or has a bike. Un-fucking-believable."

He had decimated the plateful of food between exclamations and was sopping up the last of the chile with a sopapilla.

"Hey, *¿mas café, por favor?*" he called out to the busser, who complied a few minutes later. "Shit, this is probably the worst coffee I ever drank, but right now I could drink dishwater and it'd taste great, you know what I mean?"

His eyes were shining. Camelia could think of nothing to say. She had floated up to the ceiling, leaving her body to sit at the table across from a hungry, talkative stranger. He tossed a crumpled wad of bills on the table.

"Let's get out of here, darlin', what do you say? I gotta figure some things out. I should probably get my truck. Maybe I should go to the mall or something and get some clothes, huh? Shelley probably thought I was a total bum. She said to come at eight; what time does a little kid go to bed, anyway? I don't want to miss seeing him if I'm going to go over there, you know? What is it, two? I've got some time."

Camelia had idly begun to smooth out the cash he had been so careless with, slowly unfolding the bills and spreading out their creases. She was particularly interested in lining up their edges, and when the waitress dropped the check on the table, she counted out the total and a tip with great care, then pushed a few dollars back across the table to Eric.

"Yeah, let's go. I have a lot to do, too." She pulled her coat on and headed out of the restaurant without waiting for him.

I'll look for a job tomorrow, she promised herself as she drove them back to her house while he chattered about his son, his fingers drumming on the dashboard, his knee bobbing. She would get herself back on track and try to get out of here by June.

Reports throughout the winter had forecast another hot, dry summer coming up. After last year's drought with its searing heat—the wildfires in the national forests surrounding the city, carrying a bucket out of her shower every day like a refugee, just to water a tiny patch of flowers—she didn't think she could bear it again. The wild grasses had fried to tufts of crunchy gray; the dust from the unpaved roads rose in clouds and hovered at eye level long after cars had gone by. Smoke from the fires in the mountains near the lab, where the atomic bomb was born and poisonous chemicals were buried in the dirt, filtered the sun to an eerie, muted orange. Ash fell on her patio like snow, and everyone worried about radioactivity, contaminated watersheds, toxic runoff.

Her Wagoneer swerved in the mud as she pulled into the driveway. She didn't have to stay here; there truly was nothing holding her here any longer. They walked in silence to the front door. Maybe she *could* go back to Dos Palmas and run the hotel for Chris and Melanie while they sorted out their lives. Of course, Eric would be in Santa Fe with his family; what would be the point of her being there if he was up here?

And he was right about taking her problems with her. She was sure she had heard that before. Obviously she had to finish things with Michael before she could do anything. He wouldn't be hard to find; he was probably in his apartment at this moment. Maybe she should just drive over there right now. What was the big deal? It wasn't like he was a stranger. He was her husband, after all.

"Look, love, I'm going to go," Eric said as she unlocked the door. "I need clothes, I need . . . I just need to get my head clear before I go over there." He took her face in his hands. She heard him say "space" and "time," she felt his lips lightly on hers, she heard his truck rev up in the driveway and muck its way onto the slick road.

She would move away tomorrow if she had someplace else to go.

20 *What He Already Knew*

Eric's new clothes felt awkward; the jeans were stiff and heavy, the flannel shirt too warm. He was weighed down by too much fabric. Driving through his old neighborhood on the west side of town, he had the uneasy feeling that he had never left. Time seemed to fold in upon itself. It was just another dark winter evening, and he was coming home after work, though in those days he would have stopped at the bar first, fortifying himself for the long night ahead.

He pulled into the driveway of his old house minutes after eight o'clock. Following an unnerving afternoon at the mall—so many people, and choices, and unnecessary things—Eric had driven around aimlessly for hours getting reacquainted with Santa Fe, noting what had changed and what was exactly the same. He had smoked too many cigarettes and drunk too much coffee. Now his head ached, and he felt utterly conflicted about everything. He tried not to think of Camelia at her little house on the outskirts of town right now. He had no idea what to expect from her, and that uncertainty nagged at him even as he tried to put it all aside in order to focus on what lay ahead of him right now.

The small, rundown houses still looked the same; the barrio was still the barrio. The narrow street lined with older cars, always a couple of them up on blocks, was eerily familiar. The neglected streetlights still buzzed and flickered, and the fishnet of power wires, phone lines, and pirated TV cables still wavered crazily overhead. He didn't notice how dark his—Shelley's—house was until he got out of the car and headed up the walk. In the few seconds it took to get to the front door, however, he already knew what would be waiting for him.

Nothing.

No one.

Nada.

Eric stood on the portal for a minute and ran his finger along the familiar peeling paint of the doorjamb. A jumble of footprints in the mud of the yard spelled it out, just in case he missed it. His heart fell somewhere down near his feet. If she had stood there with a sword slicing into his chest, she couldn't have hurt him more. He leaned against the door for a minute and almost fell as it swung open. The stove light from the kitchen threw a faint glow across the tiny living room. Eric stepped inside. An empty box sat in the middle of the floor. Some newspapers were strewn about, a broom stood in the corner, the remains of a fire still smoldered in the fireplace. It had been a hasty departure, he was certain, but she had gotten everything out.

He walked through the house turning on lights, his vision blurred with hot tears that refused to spill. He pushed on their old bedroom door; the hinges still squeaked. Directly opposite it was Zane's room, empty as the rest of the house. A cloud began to gather inside him, a thunderhead of rage. But there was nothing to break, no bookshelf to turn over, no plates to smash. His fists clenched until they ached. A green plastic soldier on the floor caught his eye, and he scooped it up and thrust it into his pocket, his fingers kneading the hard plastic. He went through the kitchen to the little back room he had used for his woodwork and, later, where he had slept when Shelley made it clear she no longer wanted him in her bed, especially not after Zane had come to the bed as an infant and never seemed to leave. That room, too, was empty.

In the kitchen, a packet of papers sat on the tile countertop. Several sheets of wrinkled paper were wrapped in blue; he recognized it as an official document that looked like it had been folded and stashed away for a long time. Which of course it had, he realized as he looked it over. It was dated some three months after he had left Santa Fe. The words "abandonment" and "relinquishing of rights to property" and "relinquishing custody" and a few other assorted accusations blared at him as he skimmed through it to the end, where it was notarized and Shelley had signed it. So she had gotten the divorce on her own. She had nothing to fear from him now, yet she chose to disappear anyway.

"OK, man, take the papers and get the hell out of here." A heavy-set man with a dark mustache appeared at the doorway of the kitchen. His arms were folded firmly in front of him, the familiar stance of a bar bouncer, a wrestler's manager, a linebacker.

"And who are you?" Eric said after a minute, already knowing the answer.

"Don't matter, *pendejo*. You're leaving; don't make me fuck you up."

Eric was tired, so tired he felt he could melt into a heap on the floor. Whatever injustice he encountered in the world from now on would win; he was done fighting. He gathered up the papers and raised his hands slightly in the universal symbol of resignation and surrender. The cloud of rage in his gut dissipated into a squirm of indigestion; if he left quietly now he might be able to make it back to the car without throwing up.

"No problemo, bro, I'm going, I'm going."

The man stepped out of the doorway to let Eric pass; Eric considered himself supremely lucky to be able to walk out of the house without getting pummeled just for the sport of it.

"Cool. I'll just wait until you drive away, man, and don't come back. You lost your chance; they're gone, and you're never going to find them. So don't try, got it?"

"Yeah, yeah, I got it, motherfucker," he mumbled as he slammed his pickup door and revved the engine. Minutes later he was sitting at the bar at Evangelo's, the last biker bar in Santa Fe and the only place he knew he could go right now and feel at home in his skin.

Welcome back to Santa Fe, he toasted himself as he downed a shot of tequila and then another. The liquor burned its way down into his gut, turning everything inside him into ash. He should call Camelia. He had to talk to her, to tell her something, to tell her—he didn't know what to tell her.

No, what he needed was another shot. Then everything else would go away: the empty house, the forlorn broom, the little green plastic soldier now sitting on the bar in front of him. How could this be all he had left, when just this morning . . .

"Last call, closing time!" the bartender called out, filling a few more glasses.

But he'd just gotten here; it couldn't be past nine. He looked around. The bar had been busy when he first walked in. There had been music; he remembered a jukebox that had to be kicked to get it started. The jukebox was silent; the few remaining drinkers blurred around the edges. He started riffling through the stiff pockets of his new jeans, the heavy twill jacket, looking for Camelia's phone number. He knew he had written it down. Hadn't he? The bartender came by with the bottle of tequila, raising it toward him. "*¿Uno más?* One for the road?"

"*Sí*, why the fuck not?" he said, still reaching into unfamiliar pockets. "Hey, you got a phone book?"

"Make it quick, *hermano*, it's time to go," Patricio said, tossing a dog-eared book on the bar.

Eric put his hand on the book but didn't open it. He picked up the shot and poured it in his mouth without tasting it. He heard the comforting sound of the waves breaking on the beach, he felt the warm sand of Dos Palmas under his bare feet, and he fell backwards to the floor.

21 The Key's Under the Mat

Some people face their demons; others hide from them. Sometimes, the ones who hide are the first ones to step up when the time comes, surprising everyone. The storm was over, and life went on. Camelia knew Eric was going to do exactly what he said he would, what he had told her he decided to do when he first got in his truck in the quiet predawn hours after leaving her bed that night at the Paloma Blanca. She, too, was tired of hiding. She would walk into her house and start at square one; there was nothing else left for her to do.

The level of neglect her cozy casita had endured over the past several months of her disintegrating marriage caught Camelia by surprise. Apparently, she had been hiding longer than she thought. Kitchen cabinets were dusty inside, sticky on the outside; the refrigerator harbored several unidentifiable and long dried-up spills, and some of her favorite books had cobwebs on them. Michael's rampage while she was gone had only exposed a more obvious truth: even though he was the one staying in his own apartment, she hadn't really been there at home for a long time.

Camelia had always loved this little house. When she and Michael got married, there was no question they would live there, even though at the last minute Michael told her he had decided to keep the apartment in town as well. In a way, she couldn't blame him now for having held onto his own place; she felt the same way about hers. But now, damp rag in hand, she looked at the house with a critical eye. It was smaller than she would have liked, and it had more than its share of flaws. As a rental, it would probably feel temporary no matter how long she stayed. Her landlord could wander over any day and tell her his sister needed a place to live, and she'd have thirty days to find something else.

The empty lots in the neighborhood, untouched perhaps for decades, had recently begun filling in. The new mobile homes that popped up overnight gave the whole area a flimsy feel, devoid of the kind of soul the old adobes emanated, with their mature trees casting wide shadows across the spacious yards. And the city's sprawl was rapidly encroaching; it seemed that every week she had less quiet rural space to drive through on her way toward town, and instead endured more traffic, more fast-food places, more cheap apartment buildings and crummy little strip malls. Driving had become nerve-wracking long before Saturday night's blizzard.

Hours ticked by with scrubbing and sorting. The closet, where everything had been shoved and hidden last week upon her return from Mexico, was now neat and orderly. Finally, she reclaimed the back room. Camelia spent the evening listening to a Sarah McLachlan CD on repeat, sitting on a pillow in the middle of the room, her bookshelves neatly arranged, sorting through piles of old papers and other assorted junk. Her snug little house, her haven, felt more like home now than it had in months, yet now she knew she could pack it all up in half a day if she chose to, stick everything in storage, and move on to whatever place beckoned next. Maybe she really would leave Santa Fe. That night she slept in her new sheets, in her own bed.

Sun streamed in her bedroom window Monday morning and gave the peach walls a warm, rosy glow. Camelia woke draped in an unfamiliar sense of peace. She had had no unsettling dreams, nor had she felt alone or abandoned.

As she ground fresh coffee beans and added a generous spoonful of cinnamon before turning on the coffeepot, she felt embraced by the house, by her silly purple cabinets and her cliché O'Keeffe print on the living room wall. She ran her finger along the aging Formica countertop and gazed at the jumble of postcards stuck on the fridge. The top one, an explosion of color from the flower stalls at the Oaxaca *mercado*, was from Claire, sent at Christmas.

Of course she would stay right here; there was nowhere else she would want to be.

Her morning newspaper had been thoughtfully wrapped in plastic and deposited inside its delivery box along the road, instead of tossed into the mud of the driveway. She flipped through it quickly, just as Eric had done yesterday, scanning headlines and news briefs for anything, anything at all that was not just business as usual in Santa Fe. It was almost as if the hours they had spent at the Sullivan house Friday night and Saturday agonizing over the city's unexpected response to a senseless death had never happened. The rampage on the Plaza Eric described was nowhere to be found.

The ringing phone did not startle her. When she had gone to bed last night with no word from Eric, she had put him out of her mind. He went to his wife's house and didn't come back; she needed no more information than that to know it was time to get on with her life. But whether he was calling to say he was sorry or to say good-bye, at this moment it didn't matter. She let the answering machine run.

"It's Melanie, are you there?" Her friend's voice, gravelly with exhaustion, stopped Camelia's heart, and she grabbed the phone.

"Melanie, yes, of course, I'm here. How . . . how are things? How are you?"

"Never mind, I'm vertical at the moment and that's all that really matters. Listen, we've . . . well, Chris and I are dealing with stuff, and we've had to make a bunch of decisions, as I'm sure you can imagine."

"Oh, Melanie—"

"Later, Camelia—I just can't go there with you right now," Melanie cut her off sharply. "I need your help. I know you can do this; I'm counting on you."

Camelia sank to the floor, the phone cradled against her cheek. No, no, she could not do this, not again. "Anything, Mel, whatever you need," she whispered.

"Oh, buck up, it's no big deal, Camelia. We've already taken care of all the hard stuff." Melanie made a harsh noise, an attempt at a laugh perhaps. "Look, we're leaving tonight; if it hadn't fucking snowed all weekend we'd already be gone. We're going to Ireland to find Rayne and see what's left of this family thing we've created, or failed to create, failed miserably. Perhaps we failed brilliantly, but succeeded miserably. I'm not sure, but whatever it is, we're going to see whether or not we can put things back together in some sort of fashion between the three of us."

Her eyes closed, Camelia listened to Melanie's words with a sense of growing lightness. How odd; there was no feeling of creeping dread, no worry of being burdened by something beyond her abilities. She began to feel as though she might lift right off the floor and hover in midair, her toes wriggling gently above the ground. Whatever happened, it didn't really matter.

"Chris is ready to dump the Paloma Blanca," Melanie went on after a pause. "So I need you to go down there and get rid of it for us." This time she stopped long enough that Camelia knew she had to speak.

"OK. What do you want me to do with it?" It felt like the most normal conversation in the world to her.

"Well, go back down there and make a deal with Antonio. He's already there, or will be. He can either buy us out or sell the whole thing to the Resort del Mundo goons, we really don't care."

"Honestly, Melanie," Camelia started to protest but stopped. Why shouldn't she be able to negotiate this for them? She pulled herself up and started searching around for a pencil and some scrap paper. She took notes as Melanie went on: low to mid six figures, what did that look like; what was fifteen percent going to come out to, offered by Melanie for her to take off the top? She started scribbling, her brain firing with options and possibilities, automatically seeking out the open routes through the maze of obstacles she was sure to encounter.

"We know we're going to get screwed no matter what, but try to get a decent price out of him if you can. I know you can do this; after working for the City of Santa Fe, you should be able to wrangle with Dos Palmas with your eyes closed. We'll leave some paperwork for you here at the house. Go ahead and use the hotel credit card for your plane ticket and everything. Whatever you need, don't worry about it; there'll be a bunch of stuff for you here on the kitchen table."

"Right, kitchen table, OK, Melanie. Anything else?" She thought of Eric sitting in Melanie's kitchen late Saturday morning after returning from the Plaza, his face bruised and swollen from being jumped—or maybe he had just fallen, he wasn't quite clear; he'd made no sense at all. The endless pots of coffee he'd made. The mezcal he didn't touch.

"Yes. One more thing. The house. I haven't got a clue how long we'll be gone, but it'll be months for sure—maybe years. God knows we have no reason to come back to Santa Fe. Eventually we'll figure out how to close that door, Camelia, but right now, we just want to walk through it and move on, you know what I mean? I'm sorry to leave you with so much to deal with but we just can't." Melanie's voice thickened and cracked.

"So, if you're up for it, you can stay here," she continued after a moment, "use what you want, put the rest in storage. Have Eric move in with you if you want. Christ, it took us all weekend to figure out what the hell he was doing here after all. Shit, take him with you to Dos Palmas if you want; he knows all those characters down there. Maybe he can help you. Do whatever you want; just help us out this one last time." Her voice unraveled finally, and Camelia felt her own eyes fill with tears.

"Jesus, Melanie, whatever you say. I'll take care of it," she said quietly. "You guys just go; you shouldn't have to worry about any of this. We'll work it out. It's going to be fine, all of it. Didn't you tell me that just a couple of weeks ago?"

"Ah, *muchas gracias, querida* Camelia. The key's under the mat. Come and get it before someone else figures out it's there," Melanie whispered and hung up.

It took several minutes for Camelia to set the phone down; time seemed to have stopped. Every time Melanie called, her life zoomed off into unexpected and unfamiliar terrain. Luis and mezcal dreams and freak thunderstorms. Tarot cards and dim beachfront bars. The hypnotic sound of the rattles during that chaotic trip to the mountains of Oaxaca, easily conjured even now. Eric, that night by the pool, the scent of blooming night jasmine.... Melanie's generosity in her darkest moments astounded Camelia; she could almost hear her friend say "easy come, easy go" the way she often had in the past, a wave of her hand signifying that she couldn't really care less and what was the point if she did, anyway? Things are what they are, you just do whatever you have to do. She poured herself a little more coffee and took it with her out to the portal.

Her neighbor with the bright red snowplow rode by, this time scraping down the muddy ruts into something flat and smooth. He tooted his horn and waved. She waved back, promising herself she would stop by his house later and thank him, maybe take a bag of oranges, a little bit of the beach she could share.

Camelia looked at the mountains for a long moment. She breathed in the wintry air ripe with the sweet scent of still-damp piñon and juniper trees. It was crisp out but already warming; the sky was as clear and blue as she could ever wish it to be. A coyote appeared in the scrub over by her fire pit; it nudged at the debris for a moment, gazed directly at her on the porch and then trotted lazily across the road. She watched until it disappeared.

A battered pickup truck turned onto her road down at the far end. Even from a distance, she knew who it was.

ACKNOWLEDGEMENTS

With special thanks to Louise and Michael Roach, Sue Boggio, Jo-Ann Mapson, Barbara and Robin Cleaver, Rene Bustamente and Ana Miller, Gina Browning and Joe Ilick, and Las Writers of Cieneguilla (Ruth Lopez, Lis Bensley, Hollis Walker, Kathleen McCloud, and Julie Weinberg) for their support, friendship, and community over the years of creating this project.

Thanks also go to Lisa Lenard-Cook, Cynthia Green, and Diana Rico for their fine editorial guidance.

Deep gratitude goes out to the wise women who always reminded me how to travel light: Alicia Metcalf Miller, Sallie Bingham, Barbara Riley, and Catherine Coggan.

Made in the USA
San Bernardino, CA
20 February 2019